"You're sure about this, Carly?"

When she nodded, Pete's mouth descended on hers. She parted her lips, letting a breath out slowly as she recognized she'd been waiting for this moment since they'd first met.

She slid her arms around him and held on for dear life. Pete took what he wanted and the sensation of his kiss pulled emotions from deep within her. But as the kiss lengthened, his touch gentled, and his hands began to stroke her shoulders and arms. Then he spread butterfly kisses across her eyes and cheekbones.

"I want you," he murmured in her ear.

"You've got me, Pete." She smiled dreamily. "Or would you rather I wrap myself up as a Christmas gift and sit under your tree?"

He nudged her into the soft cushions of the couch. "No, you're just fine the way you are. In fact, the less wrapping, the better."

Carly reached up and tugged at his tie. "I couldn't agree more."

Rita Clay Estrada takes Christmas to heart. For the season of giving, she wanted to write a book that dealt with an important emotional issue: broken homes. When she attended a recent women's symposium in Houston, she found out just how many single-parent families exist today. So Rita decided to create a story about a single mother and a long-distance dad...and how the two rediscover the joys of Christmas together. Enjoy, and happy holidays!

Books by Rita Clay Estrada

HARLEQUIN TEMPTATION
313—TO BUY A GROOM
349—THE LADY SAYS NO
361—TWICE LOVED
450—ONE MORE TIME
474—THE COLONEL'S DAUGHTER
500—FORMS OF LOVE

RAFAEL'S ESTRADA

Harlequin Books

TORONTO • NEW YORK • LONDON
AMSTERDAM • PARIS • SYDNEY • HAMBURG
STOCKHOLM • ATHENS • TOKYO • MILAN
MADRID • WARSAW • BUDAPEST • AUCKLAND

ISBN 0-373-25618-3

THE TWELVE GIFTS OF CHRISTMAS

1

CARLY MICHAELS LAY on the mound of red and gold leaves, fanning her arms up and down. Their swishing, crunching sound blocked out all other noise until she heard a deep male voice speaking loudly.

"Does Sleeping Beauty fall in love when she gets kissed, or does she just slap the hell out of Prince Charming for being a masher?"

The voice was sexy and rich with humor. Startled, Carly opened her eyes, and waited for them to adjust to the sunlight filtering through the trees. Focusing on the man staring down at her, she saw the realization of her worst fears. He was drop-dead handsome—and he was laughing at her.

Mortified, she remained prone in the pile of leaves. As an escape from her daughter, her aunts and her work, she had chosen the small park behind the house to let loose. She'd thought no one would be there to notice.

Obviously, she'd been wrong.

She blinked twice. He was still standing over her, with his hands resting on trim hips and a smile wrinkling his face. His thick, dark hair was brushed casually to one side, and looked as if it had been cut at the best salon in town. "Are you applying for the role?"

His smile deepened. "It depends on the rewards."

Darn. That voice was fantastic. "What did you have in mind?"

He answered without hesitation. "A white steed that can fly like the wind and a redheaded beauty with an uncanny ability to make angel patterns in autumn leaves."

Carly knew it was time to sit up and take notice. She pulled her auburn hair back and slung it over one shoulder, hoping it looked a little less like the wild mop it usually was when she wore it loose. "Such a decisive statement. But why not think bigger?"

"I don't want to. I'm a man with simple needs. I want only what I want, and nothing more."

Carly brushed off the leaves stuck to her deep gold sweater and tried to ignore the fluttering of her heart. "I hope you get what you want. Anyone who's so definite should receive nothing less than exactly what they desire."

His dark brows rose as he extended his hand to her. "Is this to accompany the old adage, Be Careful What You Ask For Because You Might Get It?"

She placed her hand in his and felt the warmth of his clasp as he pulled her to her feet. When she was standing, he still held her hand in his, and she didn't pull it away. It felt good. "If the adage fits, wear it...."

His sexy grin widened. "I'm asking, I'm asking...."

He might be asking, but Carly had more sense than to take his words seriously. The world of princes and princesses was fairy-tale fantasy. Reality was a far different place. Just because she had been thinking of dating again didn't mean that she would be granted her wish and find a perfect man. She should be more wary, she told herself; more cautious about strange men in the woods.

Carly removed her hand from his and busied herself with brushing off the leaves from the rest of her body. She didn't want to admit she would rather stand and stare at him. And she certainly didn't want to admit that she'd become uncomfortably conscious of how thrown together she must look.

"Are you from around here?" the handsome man asked.

"Isn't everyone?" She looked around the small woods and stream that most of the neighboring houses backed onto. One of its biggest advantages was that the wooded area gave everyone the luxury of privacy while eliminating the need for fences. Although she was smack in the middle of McLean, Virginia, she felt as if she were hiking in the Shenandoah mountains.

"Which 'around here' are you from?"

Carly paused. She lived with her aunts, but she didn't know all the neighbors. What if he wasn't one of them? Although she certainly couldn't imagine him having any bad intentions, she didn't give her address out to strangers. "Pick a house," she said, laughing. "Any house."

"Unfair. I live just over there." He pointed in the general direction of what everyone referred to as the Mansion in the Woods. But that house had been empty for the past two years. The owner had died and no one had bought the place yet. The asking price was so high, there weren't many who could afford to make an offer on it.

"Do you really? Then you must live close to me. I live over there, too."

"Which house?"

Carly glanced at her watch as a ploy to end the conversation and was surprised at the time. She should have taken Karen to her viola lesson five minutes ago. "Oops, gotta go. It was nice to meet Prince Charming. After all, it isn't every day one comes along." She held out her hand once more. "Thanks for rescuing me."

He clasped her hand, but didn't shake it. Instead, he grasped her other hand and kissed where a wedding ring would have been. Carly wondered if the gesture was to let her know he realized her single status. "Prince Charmings usually get rewards." His wonderful deep voice vibrated down her spine.

Before she could protest, he drew closer and brushed his mouth over hers in a butterfly-light kiss. Warmth flowed through her blood like a summer heat wave. Then it was over. Dropping her hands, he stepped back and smiled. Damn the man, he knew exactly what she was feeling.

"A slap, I think," she said, as if musing the point.

He looked puzzled for only a moment before remembering the beginning of their conversation. "Poor guy. I guess I'm grateful I'm not him."

"Oh, but I thought you were."

He shook his head, his smile slipping slightly. "Maybe I was once. But that was a long time ago." Although he spoke teasingly, his voice had an edge of bitterness.

"What a shame."

"Why?" He looked genuinely surprised. "Girls like bad boys more than Prince Charmings. Besides, there really aren't that many damsels in distress needing to be rescued."

"No, you're right, there. We've finally learned to rescue ourselves."

"So what is an old dragon slayer supposed to do to impress his lady?"

"I have no idea," she said, fascinated by this man who was showing more and more complexity. "But I would guess that you need to find a proper dragon to deal with, first."

"I think I might have found one," he murmured.

"You sound like my students at test time," she said. "Hope you find the right dragon for you." Before she could change her mind, Carly turned toward her own home and began the walk back. "Good luck!"

She kicked the multicolored leaves as she went, making the crisp, rustling noise that she loved. She hoped it would block out the sound of the man's voice that ran through her mind like a seductive memory.

"Wait!" he called. "What's your name?"

"Damsel!" she called back.

"Damsel?"

"As in, damsel in distress if I don't hurry!"

His husky laugh echoed through the woods.

FOR A FLEETING MOMENT, Carly wanted to turn back and ask him who he was and where he was from, and was he married, single, divorced? But she knew better. Most of the good men were married and most of the single men she'd dated had problems with commitment.

Besides, she'd never been that forward in her life, and had no intention of being so now. It wasn't her nature to "come on" to a guy. Either he was interested or he wasn't. And that was probably why she had so many male friends and no romantic interests. She treated them all like friends instead of lovers. Nor did she *feel* more than friendly towards them.

"Oh, well." She sighed, already resigned to never seeing the good-looking stranger again.

Karen, her seven-year-old daughter, waved from the upstairs bedroom window. Carly waved back and continued down the path to the side door of the house she now called home.

As a single parent, Carly found that her entire social life revolved around getting Karen to and from school, Girl Scouts, viola lessons and all her other typical child's activities. What with her workdays spent teaching chemistry to high-school students and her evenings giving quality time to Karen, she'd rarely had time for herself.

This year, however, was different. Her twin aunts, Cora and Nora, had talked her into moving in with them. They owned a beautiful home in McLean, Virginia, a wealthy, prestigious area just outside Washington, D.C. They enjoyed their busy, active lives, yet had always loved the idea of having children in the house. Since Carly was their favorite niece and already lived nearby, they had made the offer, presenting it as if it were only for their benefit.

True, both women hated driving, and neither could see well at night, so having Carly available for that small duty seemed logical. And true, Aunt Cora had developed a slight heart murmur and liked the idea of someone in addition to her sister being around in case of emergency. But there were many more advantages that were in Carly's favor. There were excellent schools in the district which gave Karen access to a higher standard of education than what Carly could have afforded if they lived elsewhere. The aunts' beautiful house was big enough to allow everyone privacy while keeping them together as a family. And Nora and Cora were always available to baby-sit Karen when necessary.

Their offer had been a stroke of luck that had changed Carly's life and the life of her child. Although Thanksgiving was three weeks away, Carly knew she had so much to be thankful for.

As she opened the side door and wiped her feet on the plush piece of carpet, delicious smells wafted from the kitchen to the utility porch. The aunts were at it again, cooking and preparing goodies for their annual harvest party. Tomorrow, neighbors and friends would be coming to the house to socialize, share anecdotes and stories.

"I'm back!" Carly announced as she headed for the service stairs.

"Did you have a good walk?" one of the aunts called out. Carly couldn't tell their voices apart.

An image of a handsome man popped into her mind. "Wonderful!" she replied. "I'm taking Karen to viola, now. Back in a little while!"

"Have a quiet time, dear," they both called out, knowing she cherished the hour twice a week she had to herself waiting for Karen's lesson to be over. She read, window-shopped or, her favorite, just sat in the small café around the corner and people-watched. What she did not do during that time was grade papers or do anything else that might be connected with teaching. This hour was hers.

Carly entered Karen's bedroom where her daughter lay sprawled on the floor in front of her Barbie house, playing with her doll. Her dark auburn ponytails glistened in the late-afternoon sunlight pouring through the window.

Carly leaned against the doorjamb and watched, pride filling her heart. Her ex-husband, Ken, was just as proud of his daughter as she was. Although their marriage had been an honest mistake, their daughter was not. Every time Carly looked at her, she was awed by the fact that she could have created someone so special. Without Karen, her life would not be complete. That thought was scary.

"Ready for viola, honey?"

Karen glanced over her shoulder. "Okay. Are we getting a yogurt after, Mama?"

"I think that can be arranged."

"And can we watch the baseball game at the park? Please? It's the last one of the season for the Hitter Misses."

Carly remembered all the other items on her list of things to do. But lists could wait for a little while. Karen's big love was baseball and if it really was the last game for her favorite female softball team . . . "Are you sure they don't have a game next week?"

"Well . . ." Karen stood and pretended to think hard on the subject. "I might be wrong, but I don't think so."

"How about checking after your lesson?"

Karen pulled her sweater out of the closet. "Okay. But Mom? Don't you love baseball, too?"

"I think it's a nice game, honey, but it's not the focus of my life."

The little girl heaved a dramatic sigh. "Okay, Mom. I'll try not to focus."

Carly had to hide a grin. Karen looked like her father, but inside she was just like her mother. Dramatic, quick, and determined to do what she wanted. Carly had to keep a close eye on the seven-year-old or soon her daughter would outsmart her.

"Come on, little one, before you think of some other way to bamboozle me."

"What's bamboozle?"

"Something you're already good at." Carly laughed. "Let's go."

PETE CADE DOWNSHIFTED his Mercedes convertible as he turned into the commercial area known as Tyson's Corners. He passed the contemporary office building with the decorative hole in the center of it, and then several more tall, stylish buildings that made up the small business district. Up ahead the green light turned red and he stepped on the brake. Across from him was a little coffee house that still offered outdoor seating. It was a wonderful option on an afternoon when trees were ablaze with color, but in another week or two, sipping coffee and eating pastries outside would disappear with the cold. Right now, it looked European and sophisticated.

Then, as if drawn by a magnet, Pete's gaze fastened on a mane of rich, dark auburn hair. There was no doubt that it belonged to the woman he'd found making angels in the woods. She sat at one of the tables and held a cup in her hand, intently reading a book propped against a sugar bowl. Her features, highlighted by the sun, were feminine yet strong, her skin clear and her lips full.

He was drawn to her and for the life of him, he didn't know why. Washington, D.C., and the surrounding suburbs held plenty of good-looking women. In fact, the area was known for them. And since he was single, had old money, and moved in the "right" social circles, he was a prime target for coy glances and flirting ways.

But from the moment he'd seen her lying in the leaves, he was attracted to the woman who played in the woods like a child.

It wasn't really her auburn hair that drew him, although it was thick and beautiful. It wasn't her bright green eyes with just a hint of laughter lurking there, although he could get lost in them. It wasn't her figure, even though the fit of her sweater and the hug of her jeans told him she had all the right curves.

It was the essence of her.

The light turned green and a horn honked to let him know it. He accelerated, then turned the corner and drove around the block. When he came back to the main street and headed for the restaurant parking lot, he saw that she was gone. She'd left in the time that it had taken to circle around. He hit the steering wheel with his fist in frustration. He'd lost her twice in one day. Then he remembered and smiled. She lived in his new neighborhood. He would see her again. He'd make sure of that.

His blood raced at the thought. It had been a long time since he'd relished being around a particular woman. Occasionally, he'd had the need for physical satisfaction and even less often, followed through on that need.

However, since his divorce four years ago, he hadn't had any urge to get involved with just one woman. He'd sworn not to do that ever again. There was a small soft spot in his heart that he wanted to fill with the love of a woman some day. But he figured he had enough time later for chasing daydreams, after his daughter, Cynthia, and stepson, Ian, were raised and didn't need him anymore. Once the bitterness of the divorce had ebbed, he might consider it.

Raised an only child in a wealthy family, he learned at an early age that love wasn't something that came everyone's way. The back of his father's hand against his head had taught him that love had no bearing on reality. Love was a fool's fantasy.

His work with Castaways, a shelter for battered women and children, showed him that his childhood concussions were right. He'd seen too many terrible episodes in people's lives to believe there was such a thing as "happily ever after."

With a sigh, Pete headed toward his brownstone office. He needed to pick up some files and address a few of the thousand problems that had come up last week when he was out of town. Being CEO of one of the country's largest chains of shelters for homeless and battered women and children was tough. He was constantly lobbying for fairer laws and begging for funds to keep the doors open. He loved his job, but it sometimes got the best of him. Strong-arming wealthy people into letting go of their money wasn't easy. And it took a lot of time and effort to keep the shelters high on the public's agenda. But it was worth it. His charity was one of the most monetarily successful, contributing more than eighty percent of its donations to the cause and using only fourteen percent on accounting, administrative and legal costs. Of course, it helped that he often paid his expenses with his own money. Although he could well afford it, he kept this information to himself, knowing it could make him seem like an easy touch.

Besides, he had other monetary obligations. His ex-wife, bless her black heart, had gotten her share of blood and bones from him before she remarried three years ago, the day after their divorce was final. It had been good news and bad news. Now he was off the hook as to giving her anything beyond child support. The bad news was that Sandra took Cynthia and Ian and moved to California, where he could only see them on long school vacations and over the summer. She'd taken away the only bright lights of his life.

He'd fallen in love with his stepson the moment they met, when Ian was three years old. Almost two years later his daughter, Cynthia was born. From the first time he held her in his arms, he knew that he'd waited all his life to feel this complete. But with his divorce from Sandra when Cynthia was six, the children were torn from him and he'd felt their loss ever since.

His attitude was so bad for a while that he couldn't even look at another woman without seeing his conniving ex-wife. Then he graduated to looking at every woman as a receptacle for babies. The only problem was that if he found one to carry his child, he would need a guarantee she would live with him for the rest of his life. One ex-wife and two lost relationships with children were enough.

It had taken time, but he'd finally progressed to the point of admitting that most women weren't anything like his ex-wife. Of course, he'd never marry again, but he had come to realize that life was lonely without another person to share it with. Apparently, he'd made it through another growth step. Now all he had to do was find someone who would be in his life, yet not expect too much. His schedule was demanding, and he needed to devote time to his work without feeling the pressure of a woman who wanted more attention than he was willing to give.

It was not impossible. Just improbable.

His thoughts returned to the beautiful redhead. Her reluctance to get to know him attracted him rather than turned him off. She was obviously not out to catch a husband. Maybe she would be interested in something more casual....

He had time off in the next week and an invitation to a neighborhood party that he'd decided to turn down. Perhaps that decision was wrong; he needed to meet his neighbors. Surely someone would know who she was. She might even be there.

He smiled. He had no doubt that he would see her again.

CARLY SIPPED CHABLIS and gave a few final touches to the fresh-fruit-filled cornucopia centerpiece on the dining-room table, then smiled like a satisfied cat. Although it was Halloween, she was in the spirit of Thanksgiving. A next-door neighbor had agreed to take an excited and happy Karen trick-or-treating along with her own two children. In the living room her twin aunts were entertaining friends and neighbors who didn't have children to attend to this season. Carly had just finished the last of the party preparations, so now it was time to enjoy the festivities.

The annual harvest party consisted of a casual buffet of cold cuts, breads, salads, and wonderful cookies and desserts, which were spread on the dining-room table. A bar was set up in the living room and was stocked with several types of wines and soft drinks.

Carly was excited to be sharing the season with her darling aunts and precious daughter in a house that glowed with love. She also had a new job teaching in a wonderful school. All was right in her world.

"There you are, dear," her Aunt Cora said as she swept into the dining room as impressively as a five-foot, slightly overweight, sixty-eight-year-old woman could. The grand gesture and her black Addams Family-style outfit were obviously intended for dramatic effect. But the cherubic face behind her brilliant red-framed glasses defeated the purpose. So much for drama.

"Are you going to join us? I think you know most of our friends, and I do love showing you off." The older woman took her niece's hand.

Carly gave her aunt's birdlike shoulders a hug. "Of course, I'll meet your friends. Karen won't be home for another half hour and everything here is under control."

"Certainly it is, dear," Aunt Cora confirmed. "Thanks to your organizational skills, everything will be perfect. You inherited that talent from your mother, bless her heart, and she inherited it from our mother." She sighed. "On the other hand, that particular gene wasn't passed down to either Nora or me."

Before Carly could answer, Nora joined them. She was dressed exactly like her sister except she wore black-framed glasss instead of red. "Why are you two gabbing in here when you should be in the living area with our guests?" She fluttered like a hummingbird at a flower. "And Cora, that gentleman we invited is here."

Carly saw both of them brighten in anticipation. "What gentleman?" she asked, suddenly suspicious. The aunts had tried more than once in the past three months to set her up with a "gentleman" of their choosing. "'Fess up, you two. What's going on?"

"Hello," a deep voice said from the doorway and three pairs of eyes focused on the man it belonged to. "Is this a family powwow?"

Carly's eyes widened. Tall, brown hair with a touch of gray at the temples, a smile that could seduce a hundred vestal virgins, and one of those wonderful, square jawlines from the cover of a magazine—all blended together to form one gorgeous man. The same gorgeous man she'd met in the woods.

Her heart picked up its beat, especially when his eyes focused on her. He entered the room and walked directly to her. "So I get to meet the angel again," he murmured quietly, taking her hand in his.

"Peter, this is our lovely niece, Carly, the apple of our eye," Cora said.

His blue-eyed gaze was as deep as the sea. "Hi, Carly. The name's Pete Cade."

She grinned, feeling as though the room had suddenly grown warmer. "Hi, Pete, its always nice to meet a dragon slayer in person."

Cora's and Nora's eyes darted between the two of them, and there were delighted, albeit slightly puzzled, smiles on their faces. They appeared to believe they were responsible for the attraction that so obviously sparked between them.

Aunt Cora giggled happily, then reached up and placed a chaste kiss on his cheek. "We're so happy you could make it to our little gathering. Thank you for coming," she said, almost shyly.

"I couldn't turn down the invitation," he responded with a warm smile. "It seems only right that I should meet my new neighbors."

"And you're into doing the right thing?" Carly teased.

"Of course. That is, as soon as I figure out what the right thing is. In your case, the right thing was finding you."

"That wasn't a difficult task. You had only a few dozen houses to choose from."

"Can you see me knocking on all those doors?"

She laughed, pulling her hand away because she couldn't think of a good enough excuse to leave it enfolded in his. "I can't see you trying to find me, either, although the idea is certainly flattering."

"Flattering? Hell, lady, if I hadn't been late for a meeting, I'd have followed you home. As it was, I lost sight of you in the woods."

"Well, now you know where I am." She smiled. "It isn't a state secret."

They stood grinning at each other, and she realized just how silly they must look. She diverted her gaze, surprised to realize her aunts were easing out of the room.

Pete Cade's voice slipped down an octave. "Are you going to cloister yourself in here all evening?"

"Since I'm the niece of the hostesses, I have to help out. Can I get you a drink?"

"Now that you mention it, I was hoping you might like to have a drink at my house sometime. It's not that far away. I bought that monstrous icon on the other side of the woods."

Carly looked surprised. "You moved into the Mansion in the Woods?"

"Is that what you call it? Well, my 'mansion' needed a lot of work. I've had workmen in the house for over a month. But they're almost through now. When can I give you a tour?"

Carly worded her reply carefully. She still didn't know what this man's intentions were. "My aunts and I would love a personally guided tour. Why don't you call us as soon as the renovations are done?"

"It's a date," he promised, obviously undaunted by the prospect of two duennas accompanying her. "By the way, didn't I see you sitting at an outdoor café by

Tyson's Corners yesterday afternoon?" His low, sexy voice rasped down her spine in the most delightful way.

Her eyes widened. "Yes. But how . . . ?"

"After we parted, I was on my way in to the office and I spotted you. I went around the block, but by the time I got to the parking lot, you were gone." Humor glinted in his eyes. "Did you run off with another man?"

"No. Another woman, a little woman." She laughed. "I was waiting for my daughter to finish her viola lesson."

As if on cue, a child's voice called out. "Mama!" Karen, dressed in an owl costume, ran excitedly into the room with a bag of candy swinging heavily in her little hand. "Boy, there's lotsa stuff around here! I got six of my favorite candy bars!"

"Oh, great." Carly smiled, giving her daughter a hug. "Now I can worry about tummy pains and tooth-aches." She got up and turned to Pete, who'd become very still, standing in front of her. "Karen, please say hello to our new neighbor, Mr. Cade." Carly glanced up and was surprised to see a stony look in Pete's eyes. "Pete, this is my daughter, Karen."

"Hello," he said formally. But the gentle teasing was gone, replaced by a stiffness she hadn't seen before.

"Do you play baseball?" Karen asked.

"Baseball?"

Karen nodded. "You know, like in a league or some-thing?"

"No. But I enjoy watching it, I guess."

"Oh." Karen looked crestfallen, but not completely crushed. Since the guest didn't conform to her idea of the perfect man, she busied herself with other thoughts. "I'll be in the kitchen, Mom. I wanna look over my stuff."

"Don't eat anything until I go through it, honey. You know the rules," Carly called after her daughter.

Looking back at Pete, she was amazed to see the difference a moment or two had made. From the warm, open man who'd been teasing her just moments ago, he had turned into a distant, unemotional stranger.

"She doesn't have her manners down pat, yet," Carly explained, still perplexed by his behavior. "I'm sorry if she offended you."

"Not at all," he said, taking a step away. "Well, I'd better circulate and meet a few of my neighbors. Even though it's a weekend, I still have papers to go over before tomorrow."

She felt disappointed. "You aren't staying for the buffet?"

"No. It was nice meeting you."

With a nod in her direction, he retraced his steps and entered the living area.

For the next half hour, he spoke to several people in the room. But not once did he smile in her direction. Every look was stern, unforgiving, and distant. After a few moments, she decided to put him from her mind, glancing in his direction only by accident.

As he was leaving, she saw that he sought out her aunts. She couldn't stop herself from joining them at the door.

"We'll be waiting to hear from you about our personal tour when your house is completed." She forced a bright smile to her face. "Remember?"

He smiled tightly. "Right. I'll call when it's ready. But right now I'd better say my goodbyes."

Carly nodded agreement and walked off before he departed, not wanting to see again the coldness in his eyes. Disappointment flooded her as she realized that for some reason he'd changed his mind about her. It could have been her daughter's appearance, but she wasn't sure. Although it didn't make any sense, something had caused the man to mentally withdraw.

It hurt.

Carly brushed aside those feelings and headed for the kitchen. Karen's candy haul needed to be checked. Sexy smile and dancing blue eyes be damned! She wouldn't let Pete Cade ruin her evening.

PETE DIALED THE long-distance number and waited impatiently. It rang four times, then he heard the low, sultry voice of his ex-wife on the answering machine.

The beep sounded and he spoke. "Sandra, it's Pete. I've been trying to get through for the past week. I'd like to speak to the children as often as possible and I really don't feel like you're making it easy. To help both of us out, I just sent them telephones for their rooms. The new line should be in by next week. I know we didn't discuss this, but it's important for me to keep in touch with them. It will be easier this way, and we won't have to process every word through each other. I'm having the telephone bill sent to my office, so it won't be a burden to you. Tell the kids I hope they had a nice Halloween, and have them call me tomorrow sometime. I should be in the office all day."

2

"WELL?" CORA ASKED in a theatrical whisper. "What do you think? Do you like him?"

Carly rinsed her glass and stuck it in the dishwasher. The cleanup and catering crew had left an hour ago, and she'd been puttering in the kitchen ever since. Karen was in bed and the house was finally quiet. Well, almost quiet . . .

She'd thought about pretending she didn't know what her aunt was talking about, but she knew it wouldn't work. "He's very nice," she replied.

The older woman's eyes lit up with mirth. "Nice? A dentist is nice, honey. Mr. Cade is devastatingly handsome. What the younger generation calls a 'hunk,' don't you think, dear?"

Carly nodded. Pete was certainly that. "He's also a busy man who doesn't really have time for a schoolteacher and her daughter, both of whom don't travel in the same social circle he does."

"How do you know? I saw the gleam in his eye," her aunt persisted. "Even an old fool like me can tell when a man wants to keep company with a beautiful woman like yourself. That's no mystery, dear. That's the birds and the bees."

"No matchmaking, now," Carly said as she dried her hands on a towel. "I've got to grade some papers. So I'll see you in the morning."

"You're hedging," her aunt complained.

"No, I'm just busy." She was firm, but her light hug took the edge out of her tone. "See you tomorrow."

She left the kitchen and went up the stairs to her own area of the house. She and Karen shared a large bedroom with a bath that connected to another room they used as a den and office. The small "apartment" worked well, giving them privacy when the aunts had company or when Carly wanted to be alone with Karen.

Her aunt might have been right about Pete, but it didn't matter because he'd quickly backed off. Of course, she refused to admit it out loud, but she was as disappointed as her aunts.

She pushed those thoughts away. They weren't productive. Besides, until she'd seen him standing above her the day before in the woods, she had been happy with her life.

So what if she was a little lonely for male companionship? Everyone was lonely sometimes.

So what if there were times when she missed sharing intimacy with a man she cared for and who cared for her? Even some marriages went through periods like that.

So what if she occasionally missed having discussions that included a male point of view? She could always join in the politics of the town and hear more adult male conversation than she would ever really want.

So, why was she suddenly very aware of that hollow spot somewhere in the vicinity of her heart? She'd only sensed it twice before. The first time was right after her divorce two years ago, when she'd suddenly realized she was no longer part of a couple. But when she'd really thought about it, she'd seen that she had only ever been part of a couple on paper. In spirit, they'd always been divided. Her ex-husband, Ken, had realized it about the same time she had. Although the divorce had been painful for them both, they were basically good people and wanted to do the right thing for Karen. So, because of their mutual love for their child, they had worked together to keep their relationship with her stable. At first, it hadn't been easy to be civil to each other, but the more they tried, the easier it had become. Now, strange as it seemed, they were friends and allies of a sort.

About a year ago, Ken had found a woman he truly loved, and had married her. Now they were expecting their first child together. At that time, too, Carly had experienced that feeling of emptiness in her heart. It was a feeling of not belonging, of not being a part of an intimate, loving relationship. However, she'd shored up her smile, sent them congratulations and gone on with her life.

Someday, if she was lucky, maybe she would find someone just for her. But she couldn't wait around for life to bring her someone to share it with. She had to carry on.

When Carly reached the doorway of the den, she stopped and watched her daughter. Sprawled in front of the TV in her white flannel nightgown, Karen looked like an angel. Her hands framed the sides of her face as she gazed up at an exhibition baseball game on one of the sports channels. Carly didn't know where her daughter got her passion for baseball—maybe from a "stray" gene—but Karen loved everything about the game.

"Time for bed, honey."

"Aw, Mom, the game's in the seventh inning!" she protested without moving.

"Brush your teeth."

Her gaze never left the screen. "Been there, done that."

"In that case, you've got an extra five minutes."

"Thanks, Mom."

Carly dropped into her desk chair and opened the file in front of her. Instead of looking at the work inside, she stared out the window toward the darkness of the woods beyond. Somewhere out there was a man who made her heart beat faster. If Pete Cade could do that to her so easily, was it a sign that she was ready to look for a relationship? She tested that thought in her mind as if she were tasting a new dish. It felt right.

Karen groaned at a missed hit, breaking Carly's train of thought. It was time to forget a dead relationship and stop mourning over the dearth of men and the over-abundance of women in the area. It was time to begin dating again.

She grinned. Who knew? She might enjoy the chase as much as the reward.

PETE TURNED INTO THE grocery-store parking lot. His daily maid had left a list of items he was out of, and he decided that even though everyone was grocery shopping at the end of the workday, he might as well get it done. He pulled the list from his coat pocket and glanced over it. His mind wasn't really on the piece of paper in his hand though. It was on Carly.

All week long Pete had thought of the laughing, green-eyed auburn-haired woman lying in the autumn leaves. The image had tagged at his memory like a magnet. His immediate response to her had been an attraction to her warmth and vivaciousness. The second, however, had been to distance himself from her. She was a *mother*. He didn't date mothers. They were always looking for a father for their children. He wanted to be a lover, not a father.

But the appearance of Carly in his life had made him realize just how ready he was to be involved in a steady relationship. He needed a female companion for business functions and for those nights when he was content to stay at home and entertain.

Yes, he wanted a relationship, but it had to be casual. No pressure, no emotional stress. He'd seen enough of that. His parents had hardly spoken to each other. His father had been afraid his mother would leave him, while his mom had been just plain afraid of his dad. His own marriage had been disastrous in a dif-

ferent way. He had indulged in his wife's every material whim. But for all the expensive things he gave her,
she could give nothing emotionally in return. He was
determined that the next relationship would be different—something more for his benefit.

It would be something much better than a marriage,
with its headaches of wondering whether he was coming home to a meal or to a fight. The extremes that most
marriages went through were nerve-racking. It was a
lot easier being single.

So Pete silently thanked Carly for waking him up to
the fact that he was ready for a steady relationship
again. But not with her. Her life-style made her all
wrong for the part. She was a mother—an important
reason for staying away from her. He didn't want to be
surrogate father ever again. Besides, Carly seemed too
independent for the type of relationship he wanted. His
hectic schedule demanded a woman who could be
ready for a date at a moment's notice. And she'd have
to be content to fend for herself at business functions
while he made contacts. Sooner or later, he would find
the right woman, and when he did, he would try out a
steady relationship for size.

Yes. Good.

He removed the key from the ignition and stepped
out of his car. The parking lot was packed with cars and
people. A bite of cold in the air energized him. Next to
the grocery store was a wine shop that rivaled those
of downtown D.C. and he suddenly knew what he
wanted—a wonderful bottle of Merlot.

He completed his shopping and, on his way back out, spied a familiar-looking redhead. He didn't hesitate a moment.

"Carly!"

Holding two plastic grocery bags, she turned and searched around before she saw him. When she did, her wide smile warmed his insides. He took his time approaching her, keeping himself from rushing as if it were some kind of training. "How are you?" he asked when he reached her.

"Fine. And you?" Her response was polite and reserved. But her eyes danced with tiny lights. "Have you finished your remodeling yet?"

"Almost. And have you found Prince Charming yet?"

"No. It might take a while." A dimple showed itself on her cheek for just a fleeting moment.

"Anything worthwhile out there?" His tone sounded derisive to his own ears, but he couldn't help it. He didn't like the thought of her looking for a prince. She was heading for disappointment; there was no such thing. Didn't she know that?

"Anything worth having is worth waiting for," she countered.

He frowned. "What does that mean?"

She laughed and the sound danced seductively down his spine. "Who knows? It was just something to say!"

A gust of chilly wind blew a strand of hair across her eyes and she pushed it away. It reminded Pete they were standing in the cold. He looked around, then down at her. "Look, there's a little bar around the corner. Have a drink with me."

Carly opened her mouth to decline, but something stopped her. She wasn't sure why she would want to be with a man who, only a few days ago, had obviously been turned off by her. But there seemed to be no evidence of that right now. Instead, his hand on her arm and the look in his eyes compelled her to linger. He'd obviously changed his mind about keeping his distance. She glanced at her watch.

Karen was at Girl Scouts, and the aunts didn't leave home until eight to attend a charity function. "Okay. I've got a little time."

A few minutes later they were seated in a dim booth, with glasses of white wine on the table between them. Their mutual silence was as loaded as their locked gaze. Pete seemed unable to keep his eyes off Carly. Being with her was like playing with fire. She enticed him, yet warning bells kept ringing. He had to keep the situation under control. "Listen," he began, "occasionally, I need a date for dinners and charity functions. Someone who can handle herself when she's alone in a group of strangers and I'm in another area of the room."

Her brows rose. "Really? What an odd need. Why have a date at all?"

She wasn't going to make this easy. Actually, he should have thought this out a little more before approaching her. But he hadn't, and he was in the middle of it now. He might as well make the best of it. "Because most of the functions pretend to be social occasions rather than business. I was wondering if you would be interested. In return, I'd pay for the necessary clothing."

He felt his heartbeat pounding in his ears and his hands were cold and clammy—like a teenager asking for his first date.

Her eyes widened to the size of saucers. "Me?"

He nodded.

"Why?"

"Why not?" he retorted.

"Because..." She hesitated. "You've given the impression that you're not particularly interested in me. Why would you want to invite someone you don't really seem to care for?"

He looked surprised. "What makes you say that? Have I been rude to you?"

She leaned back, her slim fingers circling the rim of her glass. "No, but you backed off so quickly when I introduced you to my daughter that I figured you either didn't like children or I wasn't your type and you didn't show it until then."

Pete paused. He hadn't known it was that obvious. "You get straight to the point, don't you?"

"You want me to pretend you behaved otherwise?"

He couldn't help the unrepentant grin. "Well, yes, I did."

"Sorry. You've got the wrong girl. I'm not into playing head games if I can help it. It's not profitable in any kind of relationship."

"What kind of relationship are you looking for?"

A small quirk around her mouth showed the errant dimple again. "I don't think that's the topic of discussion. Being a date for charity functions is on the table right now."

He laughed, low and deep in his throat. "Do you have *Robert's Rules of Order* in your purse?"

She gave him a disparaging look, but her delightful dimple reappeared.

He raised his hands as if giving up. "Okay, I'm sorry. It's just that you're so independent. It's the very thing I like about you. But it also makes me unsure what to do or say. Women take umbrage at the oddest things."

"Well, now," she drawled. "I wonder if you'd use them words if I was male?"

"No," he said with a straight face. "I'd have a fist to chew on if I did."

Laughing, she relaxed. Ever since they'd met they had dodged and feinted verbally, just like a couple of prizefighters. "Let's start over. What exactly is your request?"

"I need a date who doesn't expect me always to be at her side. In short, I need someone who can take care of herself and not demand too much romance."

"What a charming description of paid help. But tell me something. You're good-looking, wealthy and intelligent. My aunt tells me that you're even invited to the White House with some regularity." She tilted her head and her auburn hair fell enticingly over one shoulder. "Women must be falling all over themselves

to date you. Why don't you ask one of your girl-
friends?"

It gave him a sense of satisfaction that she'd mentioned some of his attributes. But he was disappointed
that she seemed to be turning him down. "When I ask
a woman I'm romantically involved with to go to one
of those functions, it's a disaster. She wants me to pay
attention to her, as though it were a regular social occasion."

"Tsk, tsk, tsk. Those big bad girls," she chided softly.
"Imagine making such demands upon your precious
time."

He could actually feel his face grow warm. She was
frustratingly perceptive. "I'm trying to be honest, and
you're making fun of me." He reached for his wallet.

She grinned. "Well, I guess I should be flattered. Although you've told me I'm the type you wouldn't be
romantic with, you did imply that I might have enough
common sense to stay out of trouble in social situa-
tions without your help."

"Damn, you won't give a man a break, will you?"

"Not when he's insulted me and given me a back-
handed compliment in one fell swoop. Instead, I become confused."

He felt defeated. He dropped some money on the table between them and pushed back his chair. She didn't
move. She didn't say a word. Instead of storming out
as he'd planned, he stopped and stared at her. Her expression was without mirth, her eyes watching his every

move as if memorizing him. "Why are you acting this way?" he finally found the nerve to ask.

Carly shook her head wearily. "I just don't understand you. All I do know is you're not the type of man for me. But, you…" She didn't continue and he waited in the silence. There were so many questions on the tip of his tongue. Still he waited.

She sighed and pushed back a strand of hair. "I've decided to look into dating again. It just so happened that you were there when I decided this. But your behavior was like a dash of icy water in my face. I resent that you reminded me just how hard it is in the dating arena, how difficult it is for a mother to adjust to the singles scene."

It was his turn to be silent, but only because he didn't know what to say. He suddenly realized how much his actions had hurt her—something he hadn't meant to do. He was too cynical and had been alone so long he'd stopped feeling the need to explain his actions to anyone, but she deserved an explanation. "I'm sorry I acted that way. I didn't set out to hurt you, but you see, you're a mother…."

"How observant," she said dryly.

He gave her a look of frustration. "And I promised myself that I would never date a woman with a ready-made family again. It's too hard when— Besides, I have my own children to be a father to."

"If that's how you feel, then I guess it's good you warn women ahead of time."

He should have known how despicable his confession would sound. Until now, he'd never put it into words. If she hadn't been so open and honest, he probably wouldn't have expressed it at all. "Just for the record and before you think I'm a complete jerk, I'll try to explain. I have a nine-year-old daughter I adore, and a thirteen-year-old stepson I fell in love with the first time we met." He stared down at his drink before continuing. It took every bit of courage he had to air something so deeply personal; something that hurt so badly most of the time, he kept it buried. For some unknown reason he wanted this woman to understand. "When my wife left, she took the children with her. I tried for joint custody, but by that time, she'd remarried and moved to California to live with her new husband. Now my children have a new father, and I can't see them other than during school vacations. Occasionally I take off a day or two and fly out to see them, but it's not the same. I want them here, but their mother doesn't like them to fly alone. So I'm stuck unless I want to take it to court, and I won't put the kids through even more emotional trauma."

After a brief silence he looked up at her and realized her eyes were glazed with tears. She reached out and covered his hand with the comforting warmth of hers, then gave a squeeze. "I'm so sorry."

It was the touch that he'd needed so badly, the womanly stroke that he missed most. The hand told him that even though his words could never fully explain the heartache he felt, she understood. "So am I. But it taught me a few things. I'll never again became involved in a relationship that makes me part of a family, unless I know for certain it's going to be permanent. Unfortunately my divorce taught me that no relationship is guaranteed."

Carly pulled her hand back and Pete sensed her mental withdrawal. He wished he could retract his words. But it was too late.

"Well, I'm not sure I understand you, but I get the message loud and clear." Carly rose and began rummaging through her purse.

"What are you doing?"

"Looking for the cost of my drink."

He covered her hand with his. "I invited. I buy."

She stopped searching, and a small smile formed on her full lips. "Thank you. I'm just relearning all the rules of dating, you see."

"It's very simple. Be honest. Be sincere. Don't pretend you can put more into a relationship than you're able."

"Simple, direct and to the point." Her smile faltered just a little.

She dropped her hand to her side and Pete felt saddened by the loss of her touch. "Well, what do you say?" he prompted.

"No, thank you."

"To what?"

She took a deep sigh. "To everything, Mr. Cade. Contrary to your beliefs, I'm not looking for a father for my child. She already has one who loves her very much. But I will not be with anyone who doesn't have her best interests at heart. Karen deserves better and so do I. And since you fit that category, I'll stay out of your personal life and expect the same from you."

Carly rose and walked halfway to the door before Pete called to her. "Carly? What would you have said if I'd told you I thought your daughter was darling?"

She turned slowly around and cocked her head as she stared at him thoughtfully. "I would have said you show great taste, Mr. Cade."

"And . . . ?"

Carly shrugged. "And what?"

Pete knew when to back off. "And I'll be seeing you soon."

As she turned her back to him, he heard her say, "Don't count on it, Pete."

Before he could think of a response, she was gone. Several men at the bar had turned to listen to their exchange, but at his direct look, they turned back and resumed their own conversations.

Pete slipped his legs under the table again and stared into his untouched drink.

She'd told him off good and proper, with all the justification in the world. He'd deserved every barb that she could inflict. It was a tacky way to act. He deserved a kick in the butt for the way he'd treated her.

But he'd met a special woman whom he'd instantly felt attracted to and hadn't been prepared for a child to enter the picture. Instead of rolling with the unexpected complication, he had withdrawn and hurt her in the process.

So? A cynical part of his brain questioned. No one gave a second thought to hurting you. No one cared when you lost your children to a damned stranger!

But Pete knew that wasn't the real problem. What really bothered him was that, although his children loved him, they also loved and accepted the other man so readily. Children adjusted quickly to change. But he hadn't adapted to losing his family. He resented it. He'd worked so hard, loved so much, been hurt even more. And after four years, the same question still battered at his emotions: If he'd done everything right, why had he lost what meant the most to him? Why had he lost his children? Was there something wrong with *him?* What made him so unlovable? He'd lost the love of his parents, his wife, his kids . . .

He squelched that thought quickly. It didn't do him any good to consider it. *Change the subject, Cade. Think of something else.*

He remembered Carly's little girl dressed in her owl costume. Her dark auburn hair, textured so like her mother's, her bright face alive with eagerness. She was so earnest when she'd questioned him about baseball. Baseball!

No. There was no way he would become entangled with a woman like Carly whose motherhood was obviously so important to her. Everything, including him, would come second. That had been his place in every relationship. But no more. Never. Nada. No way.

Pete didn't need to finish his drink to know it was time to leave. He slipped an extra dollar on the table and walked out. A big hot-air balloon in the shape of a turkey floated above the grocery-store parking lot. He stared up at it, hating everything it symbolized—family get-togethers, visiting relatives and loved ones to share the occasion with. Knowing Christmas was around the corner, he also realized it was going to get worse.

He hated the holidays, especially Christmas. As a child it had meant his father home all day and the big man's attention even more focused on him or his mother. No matter how hard they tried to appease him, his dad would lose control over some small thing, and he and his mom would pay for it.

When he was married and had a family of his own to celebrate with, for a little while the holidays were a source of joy. He'd managed to turn away the bad thoughts and find wonderful replacement feelings. It had become a season to treasure. Family. Togetherness. Love. Sharing.

Then his wife left, taking the children, and he was alone again. Only this time it was harder to deal with. As a child, he'd had no choice. As an adult, he'd found what he wanted only to lose it. In some ways, he had no one but himself to blame. . . .

So now, holidays had become the bane of his existence. Bah, humbug! He refused even to decorate the house.

"Damn," he muttered to himself, as he quickly walked to his car. He was turning into an old curmudgeon. But he survived best that way. He needed to remain in control of everything—his emotions, his thoughts, his actions. His love.

FOR HER DAUGHTER'S benefit, Carly refused to let the lump in her throat interfere with the smile plastered on her face. She had left Pete's company to pick up Karen. Judging by the painful emotions she was feeling right now, she realized she should have left earlier.

"And Cindy said that she was better'n me, so we played Turkey in the Straw to prove who was best."

"And who won?" Carly asked, trying to keep her mind on her daughter.

"Mama! I did. You know I can play better'n her!"

"Well, you never can tell. She might have been practicing, honey." Her answer was automatic.

"Yes, but I chose the song to play. I'm not gonna pick one that she can play better!" Karen sat back, a look of triumph on her face that reminded Carly of Ken. Genes were funny things, picking up oddities at random.

They drove home with Karen talking all the way. Even while Carly emptied the car and put away the groceries, Karen's childish, comforting chatter continued.

After the aunts left for a charity banquet, Carly and Karen played a board game, then they watched her daughter's favorite sitcom on TV. By nine, Karen was in bed and Carly was once more alone with her thoughts.

She turned her attention halfheartedly to a book, but by ten was in bed, watching the shadows of stirring branches on her wall.

Her mind was occupied with a man whose intense looks had made it seem he wanted her in an elemental way, but who had asked her for a date in the most dispassionate way.

Carly believed she understood what had made him act like such a jerk, though. It had been obvious in the sad, longing expression on his face when he spoke of his family. Despite the fact that his divorce was final several years ago, he hadn't yet recovered emotionally. Carly reminded herself that this lack of resolution spelled trouble for any woman who wanted more than a cursory relationship with him.

She tried to relax before sleeping but it didn't work. Over the past week she'd discovered that sleep was another kind of enemy, giving her erotic dreams of Pete Cade, promises of lovemaking that was as much tender and passionate as it was fulfilling.

Even in her dreams, Carly was attracted to him.

That wasn't a good sign....

"CYNTHIA, HONEY, THIS IS your dad. Answer the phone, pumpkin."

There was silence.

"When I had this phone installed I expected to be able to talk to you on occasion," he said wearily. "Okay, honey, when you and Ian get this message, please give me a call. I don't care what time it is. I'll be home all night. Call me, honey. Understand?"

Silence again.

"I love you, pumpkin. And give your big brother a hug from me, too. Talk to you later this evening, honey."

3

CARLY SMILED AND SPOKE pleasantly to her date all through dinner. But in the back of her mind was the determined thought that she had to have a serious, sit-down discussion with her aunts. They meant well, but she couldn't allow them to set up any more blind dates. Invariably, the men's careers were in high places but their minds were in the gutter.

This particular "gentleman," about her age, was slipping his hand under the table to touch her knee. She had managed to keep out of his reach without having to give out a verbal rebuke, but if the evening contin-ued in this direction, Carly was going to offend him.

She couldn't believe she'd let those two ladies talk her into this....

"Carly?"

Grateful for any distraction, she glanced up. But her emotions seesawed when she recognized Pete Cade, looking devastatingly handsome in a tuxedo. The beautiful svelte blonde draped on his arm seemed the perfect match for him, but judging from the expression on her face, she was perfectly bored.

"How are you, neighbor?" Carly asked with a stiff smile.

"Faring as well as can be expected." His needling gaze took in the man sitting next to her before he extended his hand. "How are you, Terrence?"

"Fine, fine. Having a delightful dinner with this delightful woman." Terrence gave a nervous laugh as he adjusted his seat to make a slight space between their chairs. "I gather you two know each other?"

Pete's look was cold and distant. Carly wasn't sure what it meant. "Very well."

Her date's laughter sounded even more nervous. But his next words showed that he wasn't without teeth himself. "Well, hope all is well with you this season. I know how the charity business is. This is a tough time with all the government cutbacks, isn't it? You must have to rely on all the regulars to keep going."

"We're managing quite well, actually, Terrence," Pete stated smoothly. "Castaways' donations come from the generosity of people around the world. Governmental politics don't usually affect our success too much."

Carly was sure that wasn't quite the truth, but she wasn't about to say anything. After all, the conversation was occupying her date enough that Terrence kept his hands to himself.

With a tug on his arm, Pete's date reminded him to introduce her. Her name was Pamela and she was very sweet. Carly wished it were easier to dislike her. After another short exchange between the two men, Pete gazed down at Carly again. "Will you reserve a dance for me later?"

Why would she bother to put herself through that torture? After all, they certainly didn't have a future together; that had been obvious from the beginning. But her mouth obviously had a mind of its own. She smiled. "I'd love to."

"Good. I'll see you later." He gave the man beside her a hard stare.

"Terrence," he murmured with a dismissive nod. The striking couple wove their way through the crowd and disappeared.

"How do you know the great Mr. Cade?" Terrence asked, a hint of aggression in his voice.

"He's a neighbor."

"A neighbor? With his money he lives in your neighborhood?"

"Yes. He bought what the locals refer to as the Mansion in the Woods."

Terrence frowned. "I remember hearing about that, now that you mention it. He took over the old Barnheart mansion and completely gutted it."

Carly looked down at her prime rib. She'd lost her appetite. "Yes. The renovations are done now."

"Did you know he chairs one of the largest homeless charities in the world?"

"Yes."

"For shelters for single parents and their children, isn't it?"

With a determination she didn't feel, Carly began cutting a piece of her meat. "Yes."

"I hear he might be a special cabinet appointee to the president for the council on the homeless."

"How nice." She took a bite of her meat.

"Some women consider him a handsome charmer."

Terrence had just won the award for making the understatement of the year. Carly was sure all women found Pete handsome. If her date had wanted her to argue the point, he was in for a disappointment. "Yes." She popped another piece of the tender beef into her mouth and chewed as if it were tar paper.

The orchestra began a soft ballad. "Would you like to dance?" Terrence asked.

It was better than sitting here talking about Pete. She placed her napkin by her plate. "Yes."

Once they were on the floor, Terrence held her just a little too close and she stiffened. But he didn't seem to notice.

"You're so agreeable. Could I hope you would continue like that?"

She glared back at him, pulling her torso away as she did so. "No."

He looked surprised. His arm loosened and Carly felt as if she could finally breathe. They moved around the dance floor in silence. When the piece ended, Carly never felt so grateful. Just as her mother had taught her, she smiled and said thank-you.

But before he could respond, Pete was there. Ignoring her date, he smiled down at her. "My dance, I believe, Ms. Michaels."

She held out her arms. Her tone was slightly dry, hiding the relief she felt. "Why, I do believe you're correct, Mr. Cade."

Terrence disappeared and Carly didn't bother observing where he went. She was sure he'd find her when the dance was over. Meanwhile, she was going to enjoy every moment of being without him. In fact, her feelings toward Pete had softened simply because he'd rescued her. She'd already been planning how to fake a headache and leave.

She loved being in Pete's arms. But the attraction was purely physical, she reminded herself.

As the music drifted into another slow ballad, Pete's arms encircled her waist and pulled her close to his lean body.

Carly fit into him like a jigsaw puzzle piece. His hand held hers firmly and his warmth permeated her senses.

"Darn," she muttered, not realizing until she said it that she'd spoken aloud.

"Darn who?" His breath heated her cheek, tracing across her ear in a seductive whisper. "And why?"

"Nothing. Just darn."

A moment went by as she flowed over the dance floor in his embrace. "Damn," he murmured.

"Damn what or who?"

"We shouldn't have done this."

She knew how he felt. Erotic dreams could have cooled easier if she'd never been in his arms. But now that she was, her imagination was running rampant.

His jaw touched her temple, and it took every ounce of restraint she had not to bury her face in his shoulder. His voice, though close to a whisper, reverberated through her body. "Did you know that dancing together is an indication of how well two people would make love?"

"Really?" Her voice was breathless. "Who would have thought?"

"It shows the rhythm of their bodies and how well they fit intimately."

"How do you know if they *don't* fit?"

"If one strains against the other, wouldn't you say?"

"Yes."

His hand was warm on the small of her back. His breath caressed her cheek. "And if the bodies flow together like a long, winding river, it means they meet in all the right places."

"I would think so."

"We'd be so good together, Carly, if we made love."

He'd said what she'd been thinking. Now it was out in the open. "That's why we can't do that."

He pulled away and looked down at her, his brows raised in question. "Why, for heaven's sake, when you know just how wonderful it would be?"

"Because there's no future in it."

"Can't you be satisfied with a good present?"

"No."

He pulled her back into the security of his arms again. Except that she didn't feel secure, she felt sensual.

"You are so beautiful." He sighed regretfully.

"So's Pamela."

"Who?"

"Your date."

"Oh, right."

"Right," she repeated.

Pete gave a heavy sigh. "Why is it that a man can want a woman as an end in itself and a woman needs the possibility of a relationship to want a man?"

"Mystery of the ages," she murmured, letting a small smile form on her lips. It was that exact difference that kept them apart.

Carly refused to admit how attractive Pete made her feel. At least aloud. Pamela was a good five years younger and looked as if she'd never carried a child. Sometimes Carly couldn't remember herself without stretch marks and the extra five pounds around her hips.

Either Pete Cade was blind, or he didn't notice. Somehow, neither attribute fit the man. He noticed, he just didn't mind. Meanwhile, he made her feel svelte and sexy and just a tad risqué. She loved the sensation, but knew she couldn't explore it.

"I'm going to regret this."

She sighed. "So am I."

"Can't we pretend that it might work between us?"

"No."

"You've got that word down pat, don't you?"

She didn't tell him she regretted nothing as much as having to say it to him.

"Promise me you'll at least think about a business-like relationship. After all, being with me can't be half as bad as dating that jerk, Terrence."

"Isn't that a little like the pot calling the kettle black? I recall a scene in a bar that left me with a similar opinion of you."

"I apologize for my behavior that evening. I was tired from too many business functions and you were too beautiful for me to give up on. Other than that, I have no excuse. But you have no excuse for dating that jerk." Pete kept a straight face. "I've had to tell him to get his hands off me at least a half-dozen times, myself."

She couldn't help it. She laughed aloud. He grinned in response. They both needed the tension broken, and laughter did the trick.

Then she slowly sobered. His eyes twinkled, and the humor in them turned to a spark of something else, something that looked a lot like desire. Desire for her. "Damn," she muttered.

He stared down at her, his eyes as wistful as her heart felt. "I know."

With a sense of somberness, he pulled her back into his arms and held her tightly. Only this time she didn't mind being held that way. In fact, with Pete, it was the only way to be held....

TERRENCE DROPPED HER off with a light peck on the cheek and a promise to call later in the week. She prayed this was one promise he would break, because she would certainly have to say no. With a sigh of relief, she closed the door firmly and went straight through the house to the back patio to sort out her overloaded emotions.

Standing with her arms crossed in front of her, Carly stared out at the dark woods between her home and Pete's. Somewhere out there was a bench bathed in moonlight. As chilly as it was, it would be wonderful to sit and contemplate the inner workings of her heart while the peace of the woods soaked into her.

This was ridiculous. She wasn't masochistic, and she certainly didn't believe in lost causes. Yet here she was, mooning over a man who was obviously all wrong for her.

Wrapping her jacket tightly around her, she stepped off the patio. Her nerves were strung tight and she needed to work off some of the tension. Her thoughts were flying in so many directions. For that matter, so were her confused and muddled emotions. Using the light of the moon as a guide she made her way toward the bench at the edge of the woods.

When she reached it, Carly sat and stared through the bare trees at Pete's house. Landscaping lights illuminated the back garden and the French doors and arched windows of the mansion, giving the place an ethereal glow. If she squinted, it looked like a medieval castle set in Sherwood Forest. Not a bad place to live happily ever after.

Odd that, for all his denials, Pete appeared to be more lonely for someone special in his life than she was. It was as if he'd been cut adrift, and was looking for the anchor of a family or someone else to love. She shook herself mentally. Maybe she was reading something into his behavior, something she wanted to see that wasn't necessarily a reality.

Leaves crackled and she turned sharply toward the sound. Pete stood, leaning against a tree, his arms crossed as he solomnly contemplated her.

"You scared me."

He nodded. "Thought I might, but there wasn't another way to tell you I was here without frightening you."

He was devastatingly handsome in a dark and dangerous way. His black, custom-tailored tuxedo showed off broad shoulders and lean hips. A white silk scarf was draped around his neck and hung down the front of his lapels, accenting his tanned good looks. His strong, square jaw projected determination and masculinity. And his eyes, midnight blue, seemed to look straight through to her very soul. She was caught by his gaze and couldn't have glanced aside if she'd wanted to.

Pete pulled away from the tree and walked over to stand in front of her. She didn't try to make small talk. She couldn't think of a single thing to say. Her mind was solely occupied with the man standing so close to her, and the image of being held possessively in his arms as he'd danced her around the ballroom floor.

"I was hoping you'd come out here," he murmured.

"Why?"

"I wanted to see you again."

"Well, here I am," she whispered.

He reached out his hands to her. "Come here. Please."

It was an invitation she couldn't refuse. Carly placed her hands in his and allowed herself to be pulled into his arms. His warmth surrounded her as he slid his hands inside her coat and pulled her closer. "I've been wanting to kiss you properly ever since I first saw you lying in the leaves."

"And I've wanted that too," she confided. Her hand reached to cup one side of his jaw and she felt the roughness of his beard.

"What?" He pretended to look shocked, but the gleam in his eyes told a different story. "No maidenly blushes? No naïveté? No pretending that everything is out of your control?"

"No."

"Finally, that word is used in the context I like," he growled, the gleam in his gaze turning to simmering fire.

She smiled up at him. "Yes."

"No telling me how you never should be doing this? That we're not right for each other?"

"No." She shook her head slowly to emphasize her answer. "Been there, done that."

"No . . ."

She placed a finger over his full lips, halting any other words. "Not now. But if you miss my grumbling so much, I'll oblige you later." She gave a slow smile. "Now. Are you going to take forever to kiss me or should I take matters into my own hands?"

His dark brows rose. "Can I take forever to kiss you? An hour might not be long enough."

Her mouth drew tantalizingly close to his, making each movement of her lips a feather-light touch on his. "You seem to know the right thing to say," she said huskily. "I only wish you knew the right thing to do."

"Teach me."

"It's not something you can teach. Timing is everything, and it comes from deep inside. From here." She pressed her hand on his tuxedo, feeling his heart.

"I think I'm getting the idea." His voice was low and gentle.

Her body curved to fit closer against the lean hardness of him. "It's knowing what both our needs are and meeting them."

"Lady, you asked for it. And I'll tell you, I need this more than you do," he muttered just before his lips claimed hers in a hungry, soul-seeking kiss.

She breathed in deeply, then held her breath as his mouth continued its assault. Strong hands soothed her back and waist and the intimate scent of him filled her nostrils. She loosened her clasp around his neck and allowed her hands to drift down to his wide shoulders. Everywhere she touched, muscles tightened and bunched under her fingers, then relaxed.

Meanwhile, his tongue caressed hers in gentle persuasion. When she responded with a heartfelt sigh, his arms tightened and he pulled her even closer. She felt his building need and was overwhelmed by her own topsy-turvy emotions.

When he pulled away, Carly felt an immediate sense of loss. He touched his forehead to hers. "You pack a powerful punch," he murmured. The night air froze his words into a puff of breath between them.

"So do you."

"Does everyone react this way to your kisses? Or is it just me that you've decided to pick on?"

She felt the same about his kiss, but wasn't about to admit it. "Everyone says the same thing. I'm a dynamite package."

He grinned. "I'm sure."

"You don't believe me?" She continued to stroke his shoulders as her eyes widened in mock disbelief. "Why not? I'd never lie on purpose."

His hands tightened on her waist. "Every woman lies." He saw the narrowing of her eyes and added, "At some time or another. So do men."

She expelled her breath. "Unfortunately, men and women have a habit of causing each other hurt."

"Women seem to be better at it."

"You must be kidding. I saw the look in Pamela's eyes tonight. It seemed to me that she's going to be the one to hurt."

"Pamela has nothing to do with this. She's a nice woman whom I date occasionally. We're nothing to each other."

"Really? I think she'd disagree with you."

"It doesn't matter. We're just friends."

He obviously didn't want to answer any questions to do with relationships. Perhaps it was just as well,

Carly thought. She didn't want to know his views. She didn't want to hurt, either.

Pete's eyes revealed an overwhelming sadness. Given time, she believed that whatever was between them could have been something significant. But he didn't want it that way and if she tried to pursue it, it would only end in disaster for her. Then both of them would be hurt for not paying attention to all the warning signs.

With as much reluctance as she could muster, she pulled back, dropping her hands to her sides. It was time to end this before it went any further.

"Thank you," she said politely, for lack of anything else to say.

"You're welcome," he returned. But there was a glimmer of humor teasing a smile from his lips. "Would you like to try again?"

"Try what?"

"Another kiss," he said gently. "Perhaps I can do better on my timing."

She narrowed her eyes. "Never mind your timing. It's just fine."

"Should I work on my technique, then?"

He was making fun of her. She straightened her spine. "Truth to tell, it could use a little brushing up. But of course, it's up to you."

"Do you think practice might help?"

"Practice helps everything. Why don't you find a woman you can become interested in and practice with her?"

"I like practicing with you."

"But rehearsing with one you're truly interested in is too important an opportunity to miss. Why, it's like playing with the pros in Shae Stadium, while I'm just from a sand-lot baseball team." She cocked her head and thought a moment before reconfirming her decision. "No, you need a special someone else to fill your bill. I'd just be a rookie substitute."

"So, it's not just the daughter that's into baseball. It's the mother, too."

"Mothers usually try to learn everything that interests their children."

"And what do men do?"

"You'd know that answer better than I do."

Carly's gaze locked with his. The moon shone brightly, illuminating his face. Was there really such a thing as fate and if so, was fate handing her grief in the shape of this man for a purpose, or was this some kind of bizarre joke?

Whatever it was, she had to put distance between herself and Pete or she'd wind up getting hurt. She took another step back. "Goodbye, Pete Cade. Have a nice life."

He stood perfectly still, knowing any movement would cause her to run. "Stay awhile."

She slowly shook her head. "No. I know high-voltage danger when I see it."

The moonlight was reflected by the shimmering white of his scarf, making his tuxedo seem even more black. "We're good together."

"We *were*," she corrected. "We aren't now. I won't let us, and neither should you. It would be too painful."

"Will you be my friend?"

"Of course."

"Then, come back here and let's talk about it."

Carly took another step backward. "You don't talk about being friends, you just *are*."

"Then, as a friend, can I ask a favor?" Pete's voice was so soft she almost took a step forward to hear him.

She smiled. "As long as you recognize the fact that a friend doesn't always have to grant all favors."

"Will you promise me you won't go out with that jerk again?"

"Why?"

"Because I can't stand the thought of you being with him. You deserve much better."

"Thank you for the compliment," she said, touched by his candor. But she was unwilling to grant Pete a favor so readily. "I'll have to think about it."

"Think hard." There was a hint of steel in his voice.

A gust of wind picked up the white silk scarf and for just a moment it ruffled in the breeze. Carly wanted to go to him, smooth it down, and then hold him close to her so she could ease some of the hidden loneliness she saw there. It was startling how strong that feeling was, and equally frustrating that she couldn't control her immediate thoughts better. "Good night."

Without looking back, she turned and began walking toward the house.

"Carly?"

She stopped and stared up at the moon above her, lighting the way back to Pete. She refused to turn around and see him standing alone once more. "Yes?"

"I have a funny suspicion that you're going to become my nighttime fantasy."

A flush of heat seared all the way down to her toes before rising again and settling somewhere in the pit of her stomach. "Don't blame that on me. I'm just an innocent bystander."

"Dream of me." It was an order.

"Good night." She scuffed the crisp leaves to cover the sound of her own heavily thumping heart.

All the way home, Carly knew he was watching her.

All the way home, she wished she had the nerve to turn and run back into his arms.

All the way home, she called herself every kind of fool for even thinking of falling for a man who was all wrong for her.

"HELLO?" THE YOUNG, girlish voice spoke hesitantly into the phone.

"Cynthia, honey, it's your dad. How are you, pumpkin?"

"I'm fine, Daddy, but it's late. I'm already in bed."

"Where's Ian? Why didn't he answer the phone if it's so late? He's got one in his room, too, doesn't he?"

"Yes, but he's spending the night with a friend so they could go to the football game at school. I wanted to go, too, but he said I was too young."

Pete smiled at the disgust that laced her voice. Regardless of how close he was to his sister, Ian obviously no longer considered it acceptable to hang around with little girls. "He's in high school now, honey," Pete said gently. "It's not that he doesn't love you, but he needs to do different things."

"I know, Daddy. I just wish he'd remember who has to listen to him when he goes on about Katie."

"Tell him I said to be nice. And to be patient, too," Pete replied. "Is everything all right?"

"It's fine. Mom and Troy are in a line-dancing club and sometimes they let me go along. I like to watch." Cynthia yawned.

"Your mom line dances?" He knew he sounded incredulous. He was. She would never have stooped to that in D.C. Or at least he didn't think she would have....

"Troy loves it, and so does she. So do I. When I get older I'm gonna try it, too."

"You do that, honey. Meanwhile, know that I love you."

"I love you, too, Daddy." Her sleepy little voice drifted off.

He was being selfish in wanting her to stay on the line. "Go back to sleep and I'll talk to you later."

"Night, Daddy," she said before the phone clicked off.

"Night, little pumpkin," he said to the dead phone.

4

PETE CADE LAY IN BED and stared at the full moon laughing down at him through the skylight.

The ache of wanting Carly was still with him, stronger than ever. It was even in the breath he exhaled. His mouth and tongue still felt the sweet heat of her kisses. Her scent clung to his neck and jawline, and the feel of her slim form was imprinted on his body.

He cursed softly.

He physically craved a woman who was all wrong for him. Another joke on him.

He hadn't wanted a woman this badly since a day after the first time he made love. Now he was older and more experienced and should have known better than to let a woman get under his skin so much that it hurt. Especially this woman. Everything about Carly was wrong for him, and yet he couldn't stop thinking about what it would be like to make love to her.

But it was more than that. Just being around her was enough to bury his cynicism and bring back childlike yearnings he hadn't experienced in a very long time. Things like loving, sharing, and the sheer happiness of being with someone who cares. Family. Children. Fatherhood.

No! the voice in his head shouted. Those dreams had died with his divorce. There was no use resurrecting them now. Damn it, this time he wasn't going to chase after rainbows.

If he could get Carly to cooperate and have a wonderful affair with him, then perhaps they could both simply go their separate ways when it finally fizzled out. Carly didn't see it his way right now, but there was nothing that said she couldn't change her mind in the future. He'd be careful not to upset or get more than superficially involved with her daughter or aunts. No strings. That way, neither would have to break emotional ties when their fling was over.

His frown was replaced by a smile. However, the moon seemed to be looking down at him with disapproval.

Deliberately closing his eyes, he ignored it.

CARLY WORKED FEVERISHLY to finish the paperwork she had to complete before the failing slips were sent out. She had two or three students who were borderline. Failing was such a harsh experience for those who were truly trying to learn. Then there was another student, a handsome young boy, who thought that he should be granted the privilege of passing simply because he showed up at class.

Karen was sprawled on the floor of their small living area, tapping her teeth with her pencil as she wrestled with a math problem. Hank Aaron, the cat, was curled against her side, purring like an engine. The sound of the new Bonnie Raitt CD drifted through the room.

Carly leaned back in her chair, took a deep breath and let the music flow through her and unleash some of the knots in her neck and shoulders. She glanced out the window at the night sky and realized that once more she'd been unconsciously staring at Pete's house.

She couldn't see all the way through the woods, but a light gleamed in the darkness and she believed it was from his place.

There was so much she liked about him: his sense of humor, the way his eyes twinkled when he looked at her. His size was just right—taller than she, and lean with muscle. And his touch was sublime.

So what was her problem?

It was easy, her mind told her. His life wasn't heading in the same direction as hers. He wanted no family, no ties, no emotions to clutter up his life-style.

In contrast, Carly wanted commitment. She needed a man who would love and give to her as much as she wanted to love and give to him. It was a tall order, but she wasn't willing to compromise on those needs.

But other thoughts kept crowding through, thoughts that told her she already knew a man she was attracted to, and that there was no certainty another man would come along and sweep her off her feet. So, why not enjoy the now?

Before she could ponder her decision further, she picked up the phone and dialed Pete's number. It rang four times, then his answering machine picked up.

Carly was both disappointed and relieved. "Hi, Pete, this is your neighbor, Carly. I've thought over your idea of being an escort for some of the galas, and I changed my mind. I think it'd be fun. So, if you're still interested, please let me know. Thank you."

She quickly hung up, her heart beating rapidly against her ribs. Karen looked up at her for a moment, then, uninterested, went back to her work.

Carly had done it. Now the ball was in his court. If he still wanted her as a partner at some of his social functions, all he had to do was answer her call.

"What if he doesn't call?" she questioned aloud. She slammed her mouth closed.

"What, Mom?" Karen asked without taking her eyes from her paper.

"Nothing honey. But it's time for you to head for bed."

"Aw, Mom," came the automatic response, but Karen slipped her papers inside the schoolbook. "Can't I watch TV a little tonight?"

"I'm afraid not, honey. Go brush your teeth."

Karen did as she was told, and Carly leaned back and stared out the window at the small light on the other side of the wood.

Apparently, he was out for the night. Her imagination replayed his earlier date with Pamela. Carly could see them dancing around the floor together, locked in an intimate embrace, and she felt a jab of jealousy. She quickly squelched it.

He wasn't hers.

She didn't want him as a lover.

She couldn't afford him in her life.

She'd made a mistake by calling him.

Just then the phone rang and Carly recoiled, but picked it up.

Pete's voice was on the line. His low, gravelly tone tripped her heartbeat. "I just got your message. Do you mean it?"

"Hi ... Yes," she said, suddenly feeling breathless. "Unless, you've made other arrangements."

"No other arrangements. I have a party this Saturday night at the Smithsonian Institute. Can you make it?"

"My calendar is clear, although I'll have to check with my aunts to see if one of them can baby-sit." Liar! she chided herself. She didn't even have a calendar!

"It doesn't matter. I'll hire a sitter if they can't. Go down to Neiman Marcus's couture department and talk to Shelly. This is formal and she'll help you choose something appropriate."

"You don't think I can do that on my own?"

"I can't take the chance. This isn't a social occasion for me. It's strictly business. Please do as I ask." His tone was brisk, businesslike. "I promise it won't hurt," he added wryly.

His words rankled her. The only thing that kept her silent was that he might be right—she wasn't that experienced in the ways of the truly wealthy.

"Okay, but just this time," she said, unwilling to give control of the situation over to him entirely.

"Good." Satisfaction laced his voice. "I'll pick you up at eight." He hung up.

"Who was that, Mommy?" Karen stood by her desk chair, her dark auburn curls glinting in the lamplight.

She was such a precious bundle of love. Carly held out her arms and enveloped her daughter in them. "Our neighbor, Mr. Cade, sweetheart."

"He doesn't like us much, does he?"

Carly looked down, surprised. "What makes you say that?"

"He didn't smile," Karen answered.

Carly hadn't been prepared for that one. "Smile?"

"You know. Smile?" She gave a big grin, showing all her baby teeth.

"You decided he doesn't like us because he didn't smile?"

Karen nodded.

Carly gave her an extra hug. "Well, we'll just have to make him smile, won't we?"

Karen's head nodded against her mother's shoulder. "Maybe you could tell him some jokes?"

"Good idea, honey." Carly kissed the top of her daughter's head. "Now go to bed. I'll be in there to read you a story in just a minute."

When Karen disappeared, Carly leaned back and closed her eyes. She'd taken a big step forward in asking Pete if the offer was still open. But her bold move had been worth it. Pete had said yes and she would see him again. Be with him again.

At least, for a little while.

PETE HUNG UP THE PAY phone in the banquet-room hall-way and allowed his grin free rein. He'd called home to his message center when his beeper had gone off. He'd have to listen to his intuition more often. He'd been right. When he'd heard Carly's voice, he'd known he needed to call her back right away before she changed her mind.

A twenty-piece band blared some raucous tune in the background, but Pete paid no attention. His heart was beating quickly in his chest and there was what had to be a stupid smile on his face. He hadn't felt this good in a very long time.

Oh, he knew nothing had changed—he still didn't want to be the substitute father to any child, no matter how cute, cuddly or needy. As Carly had said earlier, he'd already been there, done that.

He could waltz Carly around the floor a few times, couldn't he? Just because he danced to a tune didn't mean he had to buy the orchestra, did it?

"Is everything all right, Peter?" a voice behind him said, and he turned, his grin slowly fading.

"Everything's fine," he said to the brunette who was his date for the evening. She was beautiful, polished and had the body of Venus. But she didn't have spar-kling green eyes that laughed at him, that glimmered with hidden thoughts so tantalizingly close to the sur-face. She didn't have a quick wit and warm way about her.

The brunette was ideal for a function like this, but her presence didn't tease him with fantasies of other, more personal moments together.

"Peter?" His date brought him out of his thoughts. "Aren't we supposed to be dancing?"

He forced his mind away from Carly. She wasn't going to be something he obsessed about or even thought about on a regular basis. He wouldn't allow her to become that close.

He grinned, teasing her with a sexy smile. "I hope it's a slow dance, because I want to hold you in my arms and whisper sweet somethings in your ear."

She laughed and tucked her hand in his arm. "I can't wait. I have a few sweet somethings to whisper myself," she responded.

"Don't expect me to fight you off, beautiful. I'm not crazy."

But as he whirled her around the dance floor, an image of Carly's laughing eyes and warm smile kept intruding.

Anticipation of being with her heated the blood in his veins.

AMAZED, CARLY STARED at her image in the closet-door mirror. Karen was sprawled on her mother's bed, her beloved cat in her arms as she stared in delighted wonder at the woman who was supposed to be her mother. But they both agreed that Carly looked more like a fairy princess.

Carly had bought the blue silk dress with the diagonal ruffled flamenco hem knowing it clung to every inch of her body. The plunging neckline stopped just short of baring soft cleavage, and the gown's rich color accented the peach tones of her skin. She'd known it was sexy when she tried it on in Neiman Marcus, but she hadn't realized it was *this* risqué.

"You need a wand, Mom."

"I need a cape," Carly muttered, pulling at the neckline. "Or a brown bag to wear over my head so no one recognizes me."

"Phooey. If I look like you when I grow up I'm gonna wear a dress like that alla time. I'll buy ten of them, and they'll all be different colors."

"You can't play baseball in a dress like this, pumpkin," Carly said, her mind only half on the conversation. The other half was imagining what Pete would say when he saw her. Would he like it? Would he think it was too outrageous? Would he want his money back? Would he even want to take her out in it?

Once more she turned and looked at the back of the dress in the full-length mirror, making sure that she didn't have a panty line showing or something equally horrible.

Aunt Cora poked her head in the door. Her eyes widened to the size of saucers. "Oh, my. Oh, my!"

Carly's heart sank. "It's that bad?"

"Oh, no, dear. Not bad at all." Turning toward the hall, the older woman called over her shoulder. "Nora! Come see!" When she looked at her niece again, her eyes were still wide. "You look simply beautiful, dear. Just like your mother. It's so refreshing to see children take after their mothers, you know. It brings such joy to relatives."

Nora peeked over her sister's shoulder, her eyes as wide as her twin's. "Oh, my dear. You look just like our dear, departed baby sister."

"Is it too much?" Carly asked worriedly, knowing her mother had never worn a dress as sexy as this.

"It's wonderful, dear. Just wonderful." They both were quick to assure her, their heads bobbing in unison.

"Really?" she asked, finally ready to believe. "You're not just saying that?"

The doorbell rang just as they answered. "Of, course not, dear."

"No, never."

Then Nora rushed to get the door.

It was too late to worry about it now. The dress was on her back, the bill was in the mail, and her date was at the door.

Carly gave Karen a kiss and an instruction to scoot into bed early. Then, humming the death march, she walked down the hallway to the head of the staircase.

Pete stood in the entryway below, looking almost like a model out of some slick magazine in his expensively cut black tuxedo. His golden-brown tan was dramatic against the white of his pleated shirt. His cummerbund and tie were bright red, giving him a devilish look.

She started down the steps, her fingers clinging to the rail as if it were a lifeline. Pete was smiling down at Nora, but he obviously heard her coming, for his gaze lifted and took in every inch of her form. Feeling almost weightless, she descended the staircase.

His smile widened to a sexy grin that showed off his dimples. When she reached the bottom step, he came forward, holding out his hand for hers. "You look absolutely stunning."

She felt a blush on her cheeks as she answered his smile. "Thank you, kind sir. So do you."

Her aunts gave a titter as they headed into the kitchen to fix their nightly tea. "Have a good time, dear. I'm sure Pete will take good care of you."

"Thank you for the responsibility," he called after them.

"Don't encourage them with that male-looking-after-female bit. They'll believe it," Carly whispered so they wouldn't hear.

"I mean for them to do exactly that. After all, I am your protector for the evening."

"If you were, you'd be wearing a black belt instead of a red one," she quipped. "Although I think you'd look stunning in anything."

He gave a low laugh. "I'm not sure I'm supposed to look *stunning*, but if you're handing out compliments, I'm the first in line." He gave her an intense look. "If you're handing out anything else, I'll be the first in line, too."

He bent down and brushed her lips with a light kiss. Electricity sizzled between them, almost igniting Carly's skin with the heat of it. When he pulled back, she felt bereft. "What was that for?" she asked as he placed her coat around her shoulders.

"Because I don't get the chance to kiss a heartbreakingly beautiful lady often. I have to do it when I can."

She swallowed and pretended she had far more sophistication than she felt. "Must be the dress. Most men steer clear of my type of lady."

Pete opened the front door and escorted her toward the waiting limousine. "Why?"

"Because I'm a homebody. Someone who likes stability and security and family life." Pete slipped into the back seat after her. The driver shut the door, then went around the car to the front. A Plexiglas panel kept their conversation private. She snuggled into the plush seat, unable to imagine the difference between this and a huge marshmallow.

He gave her a wry look. "Does that mean that you'll try to propose to me by the end of the night?"

"It means that we're not meant to be more than friends, because we're not after the same things." She sounded prim, but she couldn't help it.

"Oh," he drawled knowingly. "I think some of what we want is the same, lady."

She refused to admit how very much she wished his thoughts flowed in the same river hers did. It wouldn't do any good....

She decided to change the subject. "Why are we in a limousine?"

Pete reached forward and flipped open the bar. "A glass of wine?"

"Yes, please."

With deft movements he opened the bottle and poured a glass, then handed it to her. "Because it's very hard to park and then find the damn car when there's a big banquet like this. So, it's easier to hire a limo or a taxi that can drop you off and pick you up. If I'm by myself, I hire a taxi driver I know. If I'm with a woman as beautiful as you, I show up in a limo."

"I see," she said, sitting back and staring out at the Potomac as they drove down the highway toward the center of Washington, D.C. "And we're headed to the Smithsonian?"

"Yes." Pete poured himself a glass of the white wine, then leaned back and pinned her to the seat with his dark-eyed gaze. "Have you been there before?"

"I've visited the museum. I haven't attended a party there. What is the occasion?"

"A sheik is giving a benefit for North African orphans."

"And you're going to help his charity? Why? When you have a charity of your own?"

Pete sipped his drink. "Because he may have a crew of people I haven't yet met. I could meet them and invite them to donate to Castaways."

Carly remembered the real reason he'd asked her out. He needed a date who would allow him to politick around the room without demanding his attention. "Of course."

The conversation shifted and they each talked about the week they had put in. The ride was over quickly. Carly finished her glass of wine at the same time they pulled up in front of the Smithsonian. Cameramen, interviewers with portable mikes and security guards lined the steps to the front door. Flashes popped from everywhere as she stepped from the limo into Pete's waiting clasp. He held her closely to him as they walked swiftly up to the entrance.

"Hang on, honey. This won't last long," he murmured through his smile.

"Most of these people don't know who we are, do they?" she asked breathlessly.

"Not a clue," he muttered, finally reaching the top and giving a dazzling smile to a camera on the left.

Several attendants met them in the lobby, took their coats and offered them drinks from silver trays. At first, Carly could hardly see the people for the blur of brilliant color. The room had to hold at least several hundred, all dressed in their finest. Relieved, Carly noticed a few seemed to be as awed by their surroundings as she was.

"That's the space capsule," Pete said, pointing upward with his glass. "Let's hope it doesn't fall. Half the wealth in Washington would be killed."

Carly's mouth almost dropped open as she watched the new vice president walk into the main area, his even more popular wife on his arm. Looking at Pete, she covertly nodded her head in the direction of the important man. "Is that . . . ?"

"The vice president's wife?" he teased. "You bet. And she tells jokes with the best of them."

"She does?"

Pete nodded. "Just before she lowers the boom and states what she wants to accomplish next. I have a feeling she'll make one hell of a First Lady."

"We already have one of those," Carly stated in a dry tone.

"Next election," he promised, taking her arm and walking her toward the main room. "Meanwhile, why don't I introduce you to her while she's still accessible?"

And Pete Cade did just that. Carly could barely keep her jitters at bay. But knowing that Pete was beside her and seemed completely at ease helped her keep it all in perspective. Those surrounding them must have felt she was someone of importance, for house photographers took countless pictures of her and Pete with the vice president and his charming wife.

Bells rang to signal that dinner was served, and Pete led her to their place at one of the ten large, main tables. A low, sprawling basket of fresh flowers was centered on each table, accenting the peach and green linens.

All through dinner, Pete talked to others around them. Though he'd warned her that he paid little attention to his dates, she constantly felt his blue-eyed gaze on her.

What was worse, she loved it.

By ten o'clock, when the band struck up and Pete held her in his arms for the first dance of the evening, she knew she was in real trouble. Although her mind knew differently, her body thought she belonged in his embrace.

"Oh, damn," she murmured to herself.

"You said that the last time we danced."

"Exactly," she responded.

Reason told her to stop worrying. She was having the time of her life with Pete and she might as well make the most of it.

Whatever "the most" turned out to be . . .

5

AFTER THE BANQUET, Pete escorted Carly outside and the limousine pulled up almost immediately. Pete waved the driver to remain where he was and ushered her into the back seat himself. The crowd, though still milling around the front of the building, had thinned considerably.

For just a moment, Carly leaned her head back and closed her eyes to help imprint the memory of the magical evening on her mind. She had met the vice president and his wife and had been treated like a princess. Instead of doing what he'd said he'd do and circulate without her, Pete had kept her at his side all evening, introducing her to everyone he stopped to chat with. Occasionally he would lead her to a corner where they could talk privately or he would dance her around the floor. He was droll and witty, passing on small, sometimes intimate, tidbits of information about those he'd spoken to or was getting ready to strong-arm into a donation. It was exciting to learn the "story behind the story" of some of the biggest political players in the country.

But what pleased her most was that Pete played the role of Prince Charming so well, she'd felt like Cinderella at the ball.

As the limousine glided out of the line of parked cars, Pete slid a cool, stemmed glass into her hand. "A glass of wine for your thoughts."

She didn't want to open her eyes yet. "I was just thinking how much you resemble a certain animated character."

"It depends," he mused thoughtfully. "If you're talking about Pinocchio, I'm not quite as wooden and I don't believe in lying. If you're referring to Dumbo, I'm just as light on my feet although I don't suffer from his inferiority complex. I'm occasionally a beast, but I usually recover by the time I've had my morning coffee. I don't have a genie on hand like Aladdin, and a limousine isn't quite a magic carpet, but . . ."

She noticed he didn't refer to the one character she had imagined him to be. She wondered if his avoidance was deliberate.

He leaned toward her, until his body heat warmed her skin. His breath touched her cheek, letting her know how close he was. Then his mouth brushed hers. A thousand little arrows zinged down her spine, then spread warmth through her whole body. She recognized the signals, knew the signs, loved the feeling.

Carly opened her eyes and gazed into his. "You're trying to seduce me."

There was a definite twinkle in his blue gaze. "That's right. But if I was succeeding, you wouldn't have stated the obvious."

"Why? I thought we decided—"

"What's this 'we' stuff? *You* decided we would only date," he corrected. "I went along with it. But I really wanted your mind, your company *and* your body."

"In that order?"

He shrugged. "Not necessarily."

Her breath left her in a whoosh. "A triple slammer."

"Right. What more could a man ask for?" he teased, before brushing a kiss across her earlobe.

"That's not the question. It's what more could *I* ask for? And the answer's plenty."

"We already decided that neither one of us is going to get what we want, so we might as well settle for what we each have to offer," Pete reminded her.

"Will that be enough for you?"

"I don't know. I won't know until we try."

She raised her hand and touched her fingers to his jaw, loving the feel of him. The urge to be with this man was so overwhelming, it was frightening. No matter how much she tried to write this feeling off to chemistry, it was still there and needed to be dealt with. No matter how many times she told herself not to care, she did. She trailed her fingertip down his straight nose. "Pete?"

He held still, not moving from her touch. "Umm?"

"Is it possible for both of us to be quiet long enough for you to kiss me properly?"

"As in a real kiss?"

She slowly nodded her head against the velvety fabric of the seat. "With everything you've got."

He moved closer, then stopped. "Are you going to grade me on this?"

"It's my job," she said simply.

A devilish grin crept across his mouth. He took the wineglass from her hand and slipped it into the holder attached to the bar. "I'm going for an A, teacher, so give me a little time to study," he murmured, just before his lips captured hers.

It began as a slow, seductive kiss, deliberately meant to titillate her. But somehow, the tables turned and he became just as wrapped up in the tactile sensuality of it as she was. He tilted his head, gaining greater access to the soft interior of her mouth. His hands slipped inside her coat and around her waist, his arms rubbing lightly against her breasts. He pressed gently against her body so they could both share the warmth they generated.

Pete couldn't stop. What had begun as teasing was now completely serious. The need he thought he'd stamped out earlier was back in full force, stronger than ever before. If he could have, he would have buried himself deep inside her until he was completely sated with the feel of her wrapped around him. But he knew that wasn't possible. So, he did the next best thing: he held on for dear life and tried to ride the overwhelming wave of ecstasy that flowed through his body.

Carly heard herself moan but didn't care. There was no holding back the flood of sensation that nearly drowned her. Everywhere he touched ignited a small fire. Every thrust his tongue made forced her closer to him, compelling her body to match the beat of his rhythm. She couldn't believe it. She felt under siege and loved every second of it. *Please don't let it end*, she found herself praying.

The car slowed down and a crackling sound came from the speaker just before the driver's calm voice filled the air. "We're here, sir."

Pete pulled back with a sigh. "Thanks, Jack."

Carly forced her eyes open and sat up. She looked out the window to the house beyond. "This isn't my place."

"I thought we'd have a nightcap before I took you home." He looked down at her. "Is that all right, or should I take you home now?"

She hated to admit just how happy she was that they didn't have to part yet. She wasn't ready for the evening to end. She wanted it to go on forever. "I'd love a nightcap, as long as it consists of coffee with cream." She wasn't about to mention that coffee wasn't what she was really interested in. Her real interest was too shocking for her to voice aloud.

"Cappuccino?"

"Perfect."

Warm-toned outdoor lamps highlighted the structure of the house, making it look impressive and welcoming at the same time. The entrance was a set of large wooden doors inset with beveled glass windows and topped with a fanlight. Pete punched in a series of numbers on a keypad and the door unlocked. He stepped back to allow her to enter first.

"I'm not even inside yet, and I'm impressed." Her voice almost stuck in her throat as she entered the vast three-story foyer. She was sure it could double as a ballroom.

"It's unique because of the mix of traditional architecture with contemporary touches," Pete explained. "But I call it home." His hand at the small of her back gently but firmly propelled her toward the back of the house, and finally to the kitchen.

"You, the entire Hilton staff and guests could call it home," she commented, walking over to the breakfast area, where a stone fireplace took up one whole wall.

"You're exaggerating," he said, chuckling as he filled the coffeepot with water from a triple sink.

"Really? By how much?" She surveyed the crisp white wooden staircase with the dark blue runner that led up to the second story. The white cabinets were inset with glass panels to show off china and crystal. Their brightness was accentuated by the navy-and-white polka-dot wallpaper. "Should I cut out some of the guests?"

He briefly turned on a coffee grinder. "A few."

Carly slowly turned around, her gaze taking in the rest of the room. "This is beautiful. But I have to ask the obvious question, Pete. Why? You're a bachelor, living alone, without an office in the home. You don't even have kids living with you. What's the purpose of having so much space?"

"I liked it the moment I saw it."

She wouldn't let him get away with that. "Most people like the Taj Majal when they see it, too, but they don't duplicate it. Why did you?"

He leaned back against the sink counter and crossed his arms. His narrowed eyes made him look imposing. "You're just full of questions that don't concern you, aren't you?"

"Inquiring minds want to know," she said solemnly.

His mouth twitched. "And you'll keep up the inquisition until I tell?"

She nodded, her green eyes not leaving his. "I promise."

Pete sighed. "Okay. Let me explain. I got divorced and gave my wife the house so the kids wouldn't have to change school districts. When my ex-wife remarried, she sold it before I could buy it back."

"Where was it?"

"Two doors down from Senator Kennedy's place. You know where that is?"

Carly nodded, impressed. The small subdivided area was walled in, with a guard in the guardhouse twenty-four hours a day.

"But the one thing I decided was that when it came time to have my children for the summer or holidays, I would give them the same type of home we lived in before."

"When can you give me a tour?"

He didn't move, didn't blink an eye. Carly had the feeling there was nothing he wanted to do less than show her around. Then he shrugged. "Why not now?"

She smiled. "I'd like that."

Taking her hand in his, Pete led her into a formal dining area with a table that could easily seat twelve. They continued through an archway into a large living room that, by the ingenious placement of the furniture, would seat people into several different conversational groupings. Next was the combination library and music room, complete with a grand piano and a set of drums.

Before she had time to take it all in, he led her up the circular staircase. She was torn between awe of the house and wanting to put him at ease. He seemed to be showing off and yet to be slightly defensive. She wished there was something she could say or do that would help, but nothing came to mind. They walked a few feet into each beautifully decorated, though somewhat sterile, guestroom before he led her down a hallway to the private wing.

When he opened the door to the first bedroom, she knew exactly where she was. She took several steps inside. "This is your daughter's room."

Pete nodded, his expression still cool and distant.

The entwined cabbage roses and green-leafed vines that comprised the design of the wallpaper, drapes and comforter were both feminine and childlike. "It's beautiful."

"Thanks, but I had little to do with it. It's an exact replica of her old room."

"She must be thrilled."

"Cynthia hasn't seen it yet."

If nothing else came through, the lack of tone in his voice underlined the intensity of the pain in his heart. "When will she visit?"

"The week before Christmas. She and her stepbrother will be here for four days. Christmas isn't exactly my favorite time of year, but I want to make the most of their visit. After that, I won't see them for another six months, until school is out in the summer."

Although Carly knew it wasn't aimed at her, his tone was so cold, it chilled her to the bone. She stepped out of the doorway and waited for Pete to direct her to the next room. Her heart sank as she peered through the doorway. It was a young boy's room dressed in crayon-bright red and blue. All types of miniature planes hung from the ceiling by invisible threads.

This was so obviously a labor of love for his stepson that her heart ached and she wanted to wrap her arms around Pete and give him the comfort she knew he needed. His rigidity as he stood in the doorway made her realize that such a gesture of empathy might break him completely. So she refrained. This love, this depth of emotional hurt was the reason Pete would never become involved with a woman who already had children. He knew he couldn't make it through a bad relationship twice.

"Ian's room," she murmured.

Pete nodded, his voice as tight as his expression. "Ian's room."

"Is it also a replica?"

"Almost. When they moved, he took most of the airplanes we'd put together. These are a few I had in storage."

"You worked on them together?"

"Yes." Pete's taut face relaxed into a smile as memory touched him. "We'd spend hours together in the evenings. He loved doing it and I loved helping him. For us, it took the place of watching TV."

She placed a consoling hand on his arm. "Ian is a lucky boy."

"Not really. For a while, I was the lucky one. Ian and my daughter were reasons for living. They were bright stars in a dark sky. Ian taught me that I could love and raise children decently before I even had my own." The enigmatic expression returned. "But they might as well be on the other side of the world, now."

She wanted to ask him why he had doubted his ability to "raise children decently" but had a feeling he'd close the emotional door on her. Instead, she tried to help him be more positive about his children's situation.

"You talk about them as if they no longer exist. That's unfair to both you and them, Pete. They had no control over their environment. They didn't ask for a separation. And I'm sure that *they're* not too happy with the circumstances, either."

Pete led her out of the room and softly but firmly closed the door behind them. "It doesn't matter. The results are the same."

"It certainly *does* matter, or you wouldn't have withdrawn so quickly," she challenged.

Pete opened the next door and stepped inside. She followed him, but all her attention was still on his hurt. "Are all men brought up to be stoic? Can't you guys be up-front and ask for what you need?" she asked. "Why are men so reluctant to relate in an emotional way, as women do? We're much stronger for it, you know."

"I'm not all men. Just me." As if reluctantly, a soft, sexy grin touched his mouth. "Have you always been this opinionated, or is this something you feel compelled to express only with me?"

She returned his smile. "I'm afraid I do this all the time. That's why there aren't that many men in my life. They can't afford the heat of directness."

"I believe it. If you don't mind, I'd like to take a rain check on this discussion until I've thought the topic through a little more."

Carly studied his expression. "And will you?"

"Yes."

There was nothing more she could say. Instead, Carly looked around, suddenly realizing where they were.

The master suite was a luxurious dream come true. As large as the ground floor of some homes, it had a seating area defined by a green and gold oriental carpet on which sat a cream leather couch and two plump, comfortable chairs. The furniture faced a large white brick fireplace framed with bookshelves. At the other end of the room was a king-size wooden four-poster bed that sat high off the floor. A down-filled duvet matched the pleated forest-green fabric skirting the base. White plantation shutters on the five windows completed the overall contemporary look of the room.

Carly could only think of one word. "Wow."

Pete watched her rather than the decor. "I think so, too."

She asked the one question that was hardest. "Is this also a replica of the master bedroom in your old house?"

"It's as opposite from Louis Quatorze as you can get."

She didn't want to admit how relieved she was. "How much input did you have on the room?"

"All of it."

"You did good," she declared, staring at the small paintings on the walls.

"Good enough for you to be talked into spending the night?"

Carly stiffened. She pretended to continue looking at his works of art. "No."

Pete stood behind her, his hands lightly touching her shoulders. "No harm in asking."

"No," she repeated, but her voice was quieter. His touch was soothing, mesmerizing.

"I want you. You know that," he said in a low, gravelly voice.

"That wasn't what we agreed upon." This time she spoke in a bare whisper.

"I'm renegotiating the contract. The attraction between us is the main reason we're together tonight. We both know that."

"Unfair."

"What's unfair?" he whispered in her ear. "My honesty? I thought you just said that the men in your life need to relate to women on their level. I'm only following your directions."

Although she still faced the bookshelves, she wasn't seeing them. Instead, she felt his hands as if they were awakening every part of her mind and body. It was impossible not to respond. His body was barely touching hers yet it was burning her like fire. Did he know how she was reacting? Of course he did. "Damn you."

His hands moved down to stroke her arms. "Can't we make love with all the passion we feel for each other and then go our separate ways without strings attached?"

"No."

"Why?"

"Because women don't work that way."

"Men do."

"I know, but I don't."

"Make love with me, Carly. Come to my bed and let me hold you until we both fall asleep." His whisper was as seductive as his touch. "Do it, Carly. What have you got to lose?"

A thousand reasons popped into her mind but she couldn't seem to sort through and put them into any cohesive order. Instead, her body leaned into his. "I can't."

His hands passed from her arms to encircle her waist, his strong fingers resting on her ribs for just a fleeting moment. "Forever, or just tonight?"

Carly turned in his arms, suppressing a moan of satisfaction as his arms brushed her breasts. Placing her hands against the hardness of his chest, she stared up at him as if pleading her case. "We both know I can't ask you to be around for the long haul, and you can't ask me to do more than keep this on a light, platonic level. If we go for more, both of us will wind up hurting the other. That's why this isn't fair. You know it as well as I do."

She was asking him for a logical point of view, only he didn't have one. But he wouldn't admit it.

He kissed the lobe of her ear, his warm breath caressing her neck. "And when we make love—and mark my words that we will—will you promise to be gentle with me?"

A smile tilted her lips upward. Pete was right. If they continued to see each other, it would happen. And as his lips moved to her throat she wondered, *why not now?* He would continue to ask and she would finally give in. Goodness knew that she craved being in bed with him. She was already involved with him. Truth to tell, she was falling for the man and nothing she'd done so far seemed to pull her off that track. *Go with it*, an inner voice advised. "I promise."

"And will you respect me in the morning?" His voice was thick with teasing, as well as wanting.

His mouth slid down to her shoulder and she felt delicious sensations all the way to her toes.

Why was she waiting? What was she waiting for? She let out a sigh that was both resigned and anticipatory. "I promise I'll respect you . . . tomorrow morning."

"Living dangerously?"

"I'm with you, aren't I?"

His chuckle reverberated against her palms held against his chest. "I was waiting for you to appreciate that fact."

Gently but firmly, Pete removed her clothes, one piece at a time, until she stood naked before him.

Gently but firmly Carly peeled off his tuxedo jacket, cummerbund and tie.

She watched as he undid his studs, one at a time, then slipped off his shirt. Her hands reached for his pants, slowly lowered the zipper and let the trousers slip to the floor.

His breath hissed between his teeth as she reached out and touched his flesh.

"Cold?" she asked, the touch of her fingertips so light that he felt like a shadow.

"Hot," he corrected in a raspy voice. "How could it be otherwise when I see how beautiful you are?"

Her laugh seemed loud in the stillness. "Thank you. I needed that."

"I can't imagine you needing anything. You seem so damn self-sufficient."

"Believe me, everyone needs something." And what she needed most right now was to be desirable in his eyes.

"You're so very special," he whispered just before taking her in his arms and pressing her to the full length of him. Their kiss was hot and wet, with need building over each passing second.

Pete pulled away, his breathing as rough and heavy as hers. "I didn't expect this reaction."

Carly barely formed the words. "Yours or mine?"

"Both. I knew we were combustible—I just didn't expect this."

"Congratulations. Neither did I," she whispered.

Pete laughed and the husky sound made her shudder deep inside.

"Do you always keep your cool in times of stress?"

"Always. It's the mark of a good teacher."

"Do you always return kisses with such sexy fervor?"

She tilted her head and stared up at him. "I don't know. Should we test it again and see if that 'sexy fervor' is still there?"

Walking her to his bed, Pete threw back the duvet. He slipped his hands to her waist and lifted her onto the mattress. She lay full length on the crisp white sheets and he covered her body with his.

Lacing his fingers with hers, he stretched her arms over her head and kissed her again as if his life depended on it.

Her head reeled as she kissed him back. Then she groaned when he trailed a line of kisses down her neck to her breast, then caressed the nipple until she felt she would die from the ecstasy of feeling he produced.

For just an instant, he pulled away to open his night-stand. She felt bereft until she realized he'd been thoughtful enough to provide protection for both of them.

Then, when he entered her, she knew she was at the beginning of an extraordinary journey. Holding on to his shoulders, she followed him into heaven. When she got there, her own sighs opened the gates. His thrusts told her he'd reached the same place.

Slowly they floated back to earth together. Carly realized she had never felt so complete as she did with this man.

6

CARLY OPENED HER EYES and stared at the ceiling. She blinked twice, acclimatizing herself to her surroundings. The weight of Pete's arm rested on her waist, his hand loosely clasping her breast. More intimate still was the feel of his hard body pressed snugly against her back.

It was the sound of his breathing in her ear that startled her into full wakefulness. What in heaven's name had she done?

The answer was devastatingly simple. She had willingly and actively made love with Pete Cade. She should have known better, should have run in the opposite direction, but she hadn't. Instead of running, she had put her arms around his shoulders and practically ordered him to kiss her. All he'd done was accommodate her.

She glanced at the digital clock on the bedside table. She'd been at Pete's house for three hours. It was time to go home.

With careful stealth, she slid from his embrace and picked up her clothing, which was strewn all over the floor. When she found her dress, she slipped it on without underwear. She'd be home in just a few minutes.

Pete moaned and she stood very still. He rolled over and gave a sigh. Carly held her breath, waiting for some sign that he was still asleep. Carefully, she glanced out the window to see that the limousine was still parked in the driveway. The interior light was on, which meant the driver was behind the wheel.

She tiptoed out of the bedroom and down the stairs. It took a moment or two to figure out the control panel next to the entrance. She'd hate to wake Pete up by sounding off all the alarms when she opened the door. It looked disarmed, and besides, she had no choice if she was to get home.

To her relief, nothing happened when she stepped into the chilly night air and closed the door behind her. She'd made it. She didn't know whether she was thankful or not.

Acting as if this was routine behavior, she opened the limo door and slid inside. "Could you take me home now, please?"

Jack folded his newspaper and placed it on the seat beside him. "Of course, ma'am."

Five minutes later she was in front of her own door. Civility was a wonderful thing; it made all this frenzy in the middle of the night seem normal.

Once inside her own living area, Carly dropped her shoes and gave a sigh of relief. When the phone rang, it jangled her nerves so badly, she jumped.

"Hello?" she whispered into the receiver.

"You left without saying goodbye." Pete's low, sleepy voice flooded her mind and her senses.

The cat suddenly appeared and rubbed its fur against Carly's leg. It felt soothing. Real. "You were asleep."

"You were supposed to stay in my arms all night." He sounded like a disappointed boy.

"I have a daughter who needs me here when she wakes in the morning."

"So she won't know that her mother's been out all night?"

"Yes."

"Hypocrite," he teased.

"You bet," she retorted.

He was silent for just a moment before his deep, sexy voice came over the wire again. "I really hoped you'd want to stay, at least until dawn."

"I couldn't. I have to be here in the morning." Her hand tightened on the receiver. "By the way, I told your driver to go home and get some sleep."

"I'm sure he didn't mind waiting in the driveway. He gets paid by the hour." Before she could respond, he asked, "When will I see you again?" Once more, he sounded like a little boy.

She pressed her fingers to her eyes, willing away the headache that was quickly forming. She realized she was crazy about him, and that getting into this relationship was taking her way over her head. "I can't think right now, Pete. Maybe we can see each other next week."

"Don't put me off, Carly. Even if you wanted to, you can't go back in time and pretend nothing happened.

We've just made love and you feel overwhelmed and want to run and hide."

She refused to admit he was right. "Oh, really? What makes you think you know me so well, Dr. Freud?"

"I don't. I just know how you reacted, Carly," he replied. "Although I can't say the same for myself." His voice sounded faintly puzzled.

His last words hit her. "You mean you think you're sure about my emotions even when you haven't got a clue about your own?" If she wasn't whispering, she suspected she would sound as if she were shouting.

His sigh echoed across the line. "Something like that. It's always easier to figure out the other person than it is yourself."

"I imagine," she murmured dryly. "So what are your emotions all stirred up over?"

"You," he said in a clipped tone.

"I thought we agreed to keep this on a business level."

"It's a little late for that, don't you think? "It looks like we're in phase two of this relationship, whether we like it or not."

"Which is?"

"Much more than the business relationship you asked for."

"But not traveling down the path toward marriage?" she asked sweetly.

"Never down that path, but there are plenty of other roads through the woods."

"Really? Name one." She gritted her teeth.

"We could be companions for a very long time, honey, and I think both of us would be happy with that relationship." His voice was liquid honey, thick and sweet and sexy as hell.

"If you need more privacy," he continued, "I could set you up in a home in the neighborhood, and hire a housekeeper to help you with your daughter."

She was insulted, but at the same time knew he didn't mean to offend her. He was just letting her know how far he was willing to go to have her near him. But she had to let him know how she felt. "So I could be at your beck and call, like all good mistresses?"

His tone turned cautious, indicating he realized he'd walked into a baited trap. "That's an old-fashioned word."

"But descriptive, don't you think?" she asked, brittle amusement lacing her voice. "Or would the phrase 'kept woman' be more fitting?"

"That's a little old-fashioned, too, don't you think?" he questioned evenly. "After all, just because I happen to be a man helping you out doesn't mean that I'm keeping you."

"No? What *does* it mean, Pete? Tell me so I can become better informed."

"You're angry about my bluntness."

She clenched the receiver tighter so her hand wouldn't shake. "You're right."

"Carly—"

"No, don't," she interrupted. "My head is aching, and my mind is so tired from arguing with you that I don't feel I've got any strength left."

"We can't leave it like this. Let's talk this out, Carly, so we both understand."

She rubbed her temple and wished she was anywhere but here, talking to the man she'd left in bed just minutes ago. "I understand that you don't want any complications in your life. You'd already set up those rules, Pete. I also understand that when I accepted your invitation to be your escort, I sanctioned those rules."

"Does this conversation mean that you won't join me Monday night for another function?"

She gave a laugh. "You've got to be kidding!"

"Not at all. Look, neither of us was prepared for tonight. Despite what you may think, Carly, I didn't plan it. I'm not the ogre you're making me out to be. It just happened. I'll take partial responsibility for it." His voice lowered but remained firm. "But I won't take all the blame."

Carly leaned back against the doorjamb. "No, you're right. I was as much to blame as you were. You set it up, and I walked in with my eyes open."

"Then let's try again, Carly. Let's try one more time and see if we can salvage our friendship."

He was getting to her again. Against all reasoning, she realized that she wanted it as much as he did.

"One more time," she agreed. "But if it doesn't work, we call it off with no hard feelings."

"Right. I'll call you tomorrow and confirm the time."

"Good night," she whispered softly before replacing the receiver in its cradle.

Closing her eyes, Carly tried to get a grip on her emotions. The problem was all too obvious. She had fallen in love with a man who wasn't willing to put his emotions on the line. It wasn't his wealth that attracted her, because she certainly wasn't starving. It wasn't his good looks; she'd been asked out by plenty of good-looking men. It wasn't his personality, although he could probably charm foxes from their lairs if he put his mind to it.

No. It was all those things and more. It was everything that was Pete Cade.

Carly walked into the bedroom and let her dress glide to the floor, then slipped a long T-shirt on and climbed between the cool, percale sheets. Her daughter, lying in the twin bed against the far wall, sighed and rolled over, still heavily asleep.

Staring up at the ceiling, Carly willed herself to forget what it felt like to lie next to Pete and feel his heat enfold her like a warm blanket. She pretended that they hadn't made love, hadn't shared the wonder of a one-of-a-kind experience.

But it didn't work.

Carly Michaels loved Pete Cade with all her heart.

PETE STARED AT THE PHONE he'd just replaced on his nightstand. He felt drained.

But the feeling he had now was nowhere near what he'd felt when he awoke and found her gone from his bed. Sheer panic had flowed through his veins before he had thought to pick up the phone and call her private number. It wasn't until she answered that a surge of relief had flowed through him, loosening tight muscles and even tighter nerves.

His first thought had been to curse her for being careless enough to go out alone in the middle of the night. While her phone was ringing, he'd walked to the window, realized that the limousine was gone, then breathed a small sigh of relief. At least she'd had the sense to ride home at this time of night.

But his anger returned because he hadn't wanted her to leave his bed. And his anger wasn't that simple. He wasn't sure who it was directed at: himself or Carly.

He didn't want to want a woman in his life again. He craved the calm, unruffled existence of a man without a serious relationship to hinder him. No emotional ups and downs. No worries about right and wrong things said and done. No expectations and none to live up to. No complications.

Satisfied with all his reasons for not wanting to care, he closed his eyes and pretended to go back to sleep. After all, he'd slept soundly with her beside him; he should be able to sleep just as well without her there.

It took dawn peeping through the curtains to make him face the fact that he couldn't lie to himself forever. Something was missing from his life and, as much as he liked to ignore it, he knew it well.

There was never a time that he didn't miss his kids, but this feeling gnawing away at his gut wasn't related to them. And although he missed regular sex with a woman, that wasn't the problem, either.

When realization of what was missing from his life came to Pete, it was so simple that he automatically rejected it. But there it stayed, like a neon sign in his mind. He missed the easy intimacy of living with a woman who loved him. He missed the openness of sharing with someone, trusting someone.

Oh, he knew it was probably a pipe dream for most couples, and he certainly hadn't had it for longer than a year with his wife. When he'd realized that she couldn't be trusted to keep his secrets, doubts or fears, that she blabbed everything they discussed to all his friends' wives and lovers, the honeymoon had been over.

But every time he thought that the magical connection between a man and a woman was only the stuff of romantic songs and fiction, he'd meet a couple who seemed to have found that very thing. Of course he knew better than to believe they really had it, but he could never shake the feeling that for some, it truly existed.

"I'm damn well going crazy," he muttered to himself as he turned over and pounded the pillow into submission. "Get some sleep, Cade. You'll need it."

But his mind had other ideas, and throughout the rest of the early morning, it taunted him with dreams that would never come true about a girl who would never completely become a part of his life.

CARLY HAD PLENTY TO KEEP her busy during the hectic November leading up to the Thanksgiving holidays. Aside from preparing exams for mid-semester, she had to grade all the homework that comes regularly with high-school chemistry classes.

As she usually did late at night, she gave herself a treat and went walking under the star-filled sky. Fallen leaves still rustled comfortingly under her sneakers as she took her favorite path among the hills and slopes of the sprawling neighborhood.

Carly reflected that Karen was as busy as her mother. Her viola classes took up two afternoons a week, Girl Scouts another evening. The rest of the time was spent studying, or playing with friends. After dinner, both Carly and Karen would pull out their books and papers. Knowing that each understood how hard the other was working made their evenings together sweeter.

The aunts, too, were as busy as ever. Fall and winter were the months most charities pushed the hardest for volunteers, and each of them enjoyed the socializing involved in their hobby. As Christmas drew closer, Carly realized how many such organizations needed the hard work these women contributed. Major charities called several times to ensure that the aunts would be available to help recruit other seniors. And the aunts loved it. Everyone needed to feel useful, they said. And apparently they were right, because they were very successful. They even enlisted Carly on occasion. Her job was usually something simple, like an hour of driving to seniors' homes and dropping off hot meals. It always gave her a warm feeling to do so. On many of those occasions, she brought her daughter along to help hand out the meals. She felt it was important for Karen to see all facets of life. Surprisingly, what had begun as a lesson turned into a treat. Karen loved the older folks as much as they enjoyed having the youngster visit.

But those times were reserved for evenings during the week, for early on Saturday morning every second week, Ken, his wife, or both of them picked up Karen and kept her until Sunday. Of course, it had become habit for all of them by now. But it was at those times that Carly realized just how lonesome she was for a family. Without Karen around, the house was too quiet, too empty. Someday her daughter would be grown and gone but Carly didn't have to wonder what it would be like. She'd already had enough of a taste to know: it would be lonely.

Yet none of those things bothered Carly as much as the thoughts about Pete that continuously entered her mind. She would be working away when suddenly she'd realize that she'd just spent the past fifteen minutes daydreaming about the man. It was unfair. If she wasn't busy every minute of every day, he would invade her very being, robbing her of other thoughts.

They had gone out to charity events three times since the night they'd made love. At first, she'd been awkward around him, unable to think of anything other than the touch of his hands on her skin, the rough feel of his cheek against her throat, the pulse of his body as they made love....

She'd give herself a mental shake, and chide herself, *Enough!*

But the thoughts didn't disappear for long. Like water seeping through an earthen dam, they remained just below the surface. After several weeks, however, she'd become accustomed to thinking, dreaming, and wondering about Pete. It was a new habit.

Carly scuffed another bank of leaves. She looked up and noticed that a man stood under the light of a dim streetlamp farther down the road. He wore a dark warm-up suit and baseball cap and was leaning against the post, as though waiting. But for what? It wasn't a bus stop.

Her steps faltered slightly and she cursed herself for coming out with her keys and not her pepper spray. In this day and age it was foolish not to be prepared, and she slowed her pace in order to think through her mounting panic.

As she got closer, the man stood and lifted his brim. "Going my way?"

The lamplight streamed across the strong, male features she knew so well. Carly gave a sigh of relief. "What are you doing here, Pete?"

When she reached his side, he turned and walked with her. "I've seen your routine often enough that I took a chance you'd repeat it again tonight. You should be more particular about where you walk."

"When I feel the need for a lecture, I promise I'll call you."

He glanced at her "Sorry. overprotectiveness is a habit I acquired when I was an active father."

She answered with a light laugh. "I know those feelings. I just don't want to be the recipient of them."

As they walked in silence for a few minutes, Carly realized every pore in her body was aware of the man striding beside her.

Pete's voice broke into her reverie. "I really care, you know."

Hope surged through her veins like a stream of liquid gold in bedrock. But she forced herself to remain calm. Caring wasn't even close to loving. "For anything in particular or everything in general?"

"Don't play dumb, Carly. It doesn't become you."

"I'm not playing, Pete. I'm just unwilling to put my own interpretation on your words. If you're going to say something to me, then you'd better be prepared to explain it." She looked at him with a raised brow. "Just so I don't misunderstand."

He sighed. "I'll never marry again. I'll never try to find a replacement for my own family."

The words hurt, but she didn't let her pace falter. "I don't recall asking you to do either of those things."

"No, but the implication is there. I'm just letting you know that my feelings about families and children haven't changed."

She forced a nonchalant tone into her voice. "Why, Pete, watch out or someone might think you care."

His sigh was heavier this time. "That's what I just said."

Carly stopped, a frown creasing her brow as she stared up at him. "What exactly is it that you care about?"

"You." It was said calmly, clearly, and without hesitation.

She gave a nod and turned to continue walking. "Okay. Now I'm supposed to say thank-you, I guess."

He shook his head. "Now you're supposed to stand still long enough for me to kiss you."

"You can't."

"Why?"

"Because I'm not taking any chances on crossed signals," she explained. "We agreed that we wouldn't get involved again."

He stopped her with the light pressure of his hand on her arm. His fingers slipped under her chin and lifted her face to his. "No. You agreed with yourself. I just listened." His voice dropped. "But I'm tired of staying away from the very thing I care about. I'm tired of dreaming of what we had together and waiting for the magic to happen again. Instead, I'd rather try for it once more."

Before she could protest, his mouth came down on hers, claiming her attention and branding her as a treasured possession. His hands slipped to her waist and pulled her closer to his rock-hard form. She felt every muscle, every nuance of his body as it touched hers, and her emotions reacted just as they had the night they made love. Her fingers sought the back of his neck, and she thrilled as her palms met the coarse texture of his hair.

She was where she dreamed of being, where she wanted to be. No, this was where she *needed* to be...to find happiness.

Carly dragged her mouth away and stared up into eyes that were as dazed as hers. "No. You can't do this again."

"I just did." Once again he stole her breath by kissing her, but this time he was more gentle, seducing nectar from her mouth one drop at a time. Once again she succumbed to the overwhelming feelings that he caused within her.

This time he broke away, but his arms tightened around her waist as he pulled her in against the heat of his chest. "Lady, you're amazing."

"It's my job," she answered, trying to keep a thin hold on her sanity by being flippant. As long as she could wisecrack, he wouldn't know how deeply she loved him, and she wouldn't lose face.

"Come over tomorrow night."

"Why? For what?"

"For me. For us." He suddenly smiled. "We could watch a movie."

It took everything she had to draw back. "Sorry, buddy. No dates, remember?"

"How about a pajama party?"

"I don't think so," she said slowly, sounding so prim and proper she could hardly stand it—especially when what she really wanted was to strip off his clothes and lie in the leaves with him then and there. "I think it's time for me to go home."

"Why?"

"We both know the reasons. *You* don't fall in love and *I* want a relationship. You don't like kids if they aren't yours but I love kids, have one, and want more. You're looking for a sophisticated woman who can handle all the ins and outs of your business, I want a man who handles all the ins and outs of a family."

"You don't want my caring?"

"Caring isn't a substitute for love."

"Fine. I understand. You're not willing to settle for less than what you want. I'm not willing to go the lengths you want me to."

A large lump clogged her throat. She took a step back. "That's right. See you later." With a turn, she resumed her walk.

"You've put a spell on me lady." His muttered words barely reached her ears.

She knew he watched her all the way down her block.

"SANDRA, I WANT TO SEE the kids over Christmas. Either they come here or I go there. Which will it be?"

"Peter, they really need the structure of a family at this time," she hedged, pretending to be reasonable. "Besides, Cynthia has a piano recital and is all involved in a church play. And Ian has gym practice every day after school to prepare for basketball tryouts."

"I don't care. I want to see them."

"You're supposed to see them for a month over the summer, too. Isn't that enough to fit into your busy schedule? Except for special occasions, you hardly had time to turn around and notice your family when we were all living together. You spent more time with the homeless than you did with us." Her voice was bitter with the memory. "Why the sudden interest in being with them, now that we've moved away?"

"Which will it be?" he persisted, ignoring the vein of truth in her accusation.

"Troy won't like it . . ." she began.

"To hell with Troy. He's not my children's father—*I* am. He knew that when you two met and were carrying on behind my back. He knew that when he married you the day after our divorce was final."

"Peter . . ."

"The law states I have visitation rights, Sandra. Or would you rather I go back to court and fight you on this? I can drag as much dirt into it as you want me to."

She gave a heavy sigh, and he could imagine the look that must be on her face—long-suffering and drawn as if in pain. "Fine, Peter. You may spend Christmas with the children. Here in California."

"Gee, thanks, Sandra. What a wonderful gesture." His voice was leaden with sarcasm, but inside he felt triumphant. "Have a wonderful week. I'll call you from the airport. Meantime, give the kids my love and tell them I'll see them soon."

This time, hanging up the receiver gave him a sense of satisfaction. He had won, but the feeling of triumph quickly ebbed and a wave of loneliness washed over him.

7

CARLY WAS TRYING TO CATCH up on all her paperwork. Thanksgiving was approaching and she couldn't wait. She needed the long weekend to recuperate from the hectic pace of teaching, parenting and socializing. It would also give her a little more time with her daughter.

Earlier this evening, Karen had dragged her to a local baseball game, then to a pizza parlor for dinner before the child had dropped, exhausted, into bed. Carly forced herself to sift through the stack of papers she hadn't graded yet.

Aunt Nora appeared at the door, took one look at her and decided what her niece needed was a good hot cup of tea. Obviously determined to keep her company, Nora placed the tray on a stack of tests and, giving a bright smile, sat in the cozy Morris chair that took up a corner of Carly's small living area. With an inaudible sigh, Carly realized this might be a long visit.

"We never get to talk anymore, sweetie. How is school?"

Carly forced herself to lean back and indulge her aunt for a little while. "School is fine, considering that half the students wish they had the nerve to be delinquents, while the other half already are."

"My, my, dear. I had no idea. In my day, things were so different. No one would dream of doing anything illegal. Now it seems to be so common!"

"It looks that way, I know. But that's not really the case, Aunt Nora, at least not where I teach. I'm just complaining for the heck of it."

Her aunt looked a little relieved. "Oh. Well, that's good, dear. And what about your personal life?" The older woman continued before Carly could answer. "If you remember, one of the reasons you moved here was so you could get out a little more. You know, have some kind of social life for yourself."

"My personal life is fine, auntie. I date on occasion and I have plenty of time for Karen. It's perfect," Carly soothed. "And I really don't want any more blind dates."

"Of course not, dear." Nora perked up and an innocent expression came over her sweetly lined face. "And how is that handsome young man, Peter Cade? We haven't seen him since that night you met the vice president."

"He's just fine," Carly managed to say with a straight face. She reached for her tea and took a sip. So this was the real reason behind this chat. Her aunts had decided their curiosity needed to be fed. "We've attended several banquets together but he's always been caught downtown and sent a car for me, instead."

"Are you enjoying his company? Your Aunt Cora was concerned about that, you know." Nora leaned forward and dropped her voice to a whisper. "She was worried that we might not have done the right thing by introducing you to him. Neither of us would ever sanction him not being a gentleman in every way."

The thought of his kiss under the streetlamp came to mind, followed by images of their lovemaking on his crisp white sheets by the light of the moon. Her mouth went dry at the memory. "He's a gentleman, Aunt Nora."

"When do you see him again?"

Carly pretended to think about it, although she knew exactly when their next meeting was. Every thought was attached to that event, every tremor of her heart in anticipation of it. She'd even thought of canceling because she knew it was best for both of them. But she couldn't. "Sunday afternoon. We're attending a tea."

"How nice, dear. If you're late, Cora and I will be here when Ken drops Karen off."

"Thank you, I'd appreciate that."

Nora stood and smoothed down the front of her dress. "No trouble at all. You know we adore that daughter of yours. She makes me remember my own youth." The older woman's gaze drifted off to another time. "Daddy was always so proud of us, don't you know. He used to say he couldn't wait to get home to see his girls."

Carly placed her cup on the tray. As if to brush away old memories, her aunt shook her head. She readied the tray to take back to the kitchen.

"You were very lucky, Aunt Nora," Carly said.

Her aunt's smile slipped slightly. "I know. Cora and I say that at least once a week. But we're the only ones left, you know. It's hard to realize your parents and siblings are all gone and you're the only ones here to remember. If it weren't for you and your darling one, why, we'd feel positively lonely!"

Carly was touched. She leaned forward and placed a kiss on her aunt's cheek. "Whether we're here or somewhere else, aunt, we're still relatives."

Nora chuckled and reached for the tray. "I know, it's just nice to get to know you this way. The house is so big with just the two of us rattling around. We could put four more people in here and there would still be plenty of room...."

"Are you thinking of bringing in another boarder?"

"No, of course not." She looked a little sheepish. "It was that sister of mine who brought it up. But, it was just a thought. You know, kinda like those Golden Girls on TV. They all get to sit in the kitchen and gab away to each other in the evenings."

It was true, her aunts were always ready for a good conversation, especially if it was accompanied by a slice of cheesecake. And they both loved company. Although Carly lived with them, she was seldom downstairs, preferring the quiet of her own little niche off the bedroom. "They do make it look like fun, don't they?"

"Yes, but that's not the real world, is it, dear?" Her aunt turned to leave. "But still, it does look enjoyable."

Carly's conscience pricked her. She hadn't been the best company since she'd met Pete, and maybe her aunts needed more. "Perhaps you ought to think about one of your friends moving in. As you say, there's plenty of room."

"We'll see." The older woman peered through her bifocals. "I'll leave you alone for a while so you can get your work done. Sleep well, honey."

"You, too," Carly replied, forcing herself to turn back to the stack of paperwork.

For the next fifteen minutes she pretended she was working on the papers in front of her instead of wondering what Pete was up to and who he was with.

But it did no good. Instead, after several halfhearted attempts to finish her grading, she gave up. Picking up the remote control, Carly turned on the TV just in time to see the nightly news.

After a commercial break, Carly was surprised to see Pete's face flash on the screen. His smile was charming and beguiling as the announcer droned on about a gala at the Russian embassy. Her surprise quickly turned to hurt when the camera pulled back to reveal a petite, beautiful woman on Pete's arm, gazing up at him adoringly.

Another woman. How many more were there in his life?

An ache began in the area of her heart, expanding until she thought her breast was on fire. It was no secret that Pete dated other women but, with the exception of the woman he'd introduced her to the night of her blind date, his women had always been nebulous beings without a face or figure. She had imagined none of them with the looks and style and panache of the woman who was on his arm this night. Like nothing else, the camera brought home just how much he got around. She loved him with all her heart, but this revelation reinforced the futility of it.

Granted, Pete had wanted her in his bed and he'd made no bones about it. But how many had followed in her footsteps? How many had been before her? It was amazing that previously she hadn't thought about it. But now, with the flick of a TV switch, she couldn't forget it.

Tears streamed down her face as she stared at the screen. "Damn you, Pete Cade, for making me fall in love with you. Damn you!"

It wasn't her fault, her logical side told her. But she wasn't in the mood for logic. Logic was something that worked without the burden of emotions. She was beyond that. Emotions were all she had these days.

Her mind slithered here and there as she tried to calm down. She paced the room, needing action. As she strode back and forth, her mind continued to race. What could she do? What would ever persuade Pete to care only for her?

She knew he didn't love her, but he'd told her he cared. How much, though? Enough to be faithful? Enough to date only her? Enough to love her? Enough to love? That was the question uppermost in her mind.

She had only two choices. She could either force herself to walk away from Pete and never see him again, accepting that he would never change. Or, she could try to make him fall in love enough to marry and have children with her.

If she walked away, she wouldn't have to worry about any more heartache than she suffered now. What was it fitness freaks said? No pain, no gain? Obviously, she was already hurting like the devil.

If she tried to make him fall in love with her and lost, she wouldn't be any worse off. And she would at least know that she'd given it her best.

If she didn't try she'd still be hurting but would have the added burden of always wondering what might have happened if she'd taken a chance.

Finally, with an exhaustion that permeated her very being, she walked into the bedroom and stripped off her clothes. After a few minutes in bed, her pillow was stained with tears. But by the time she fell asleep, a small smile had appeared on her lips. At least she knew what she had to do.

PETE PICKED CARLY up in his Mercedes just a little after lunchtime on Sunday. He was dressed impeccably, as usual, and she couldn't help the surge of pride that filled her as he walked her to his car and opened the door for her.

Once they were on their way down the freeway, she turned casually and placed her hand on his arm to gain his attention. "Do you remember the discussion we had on my being in your bed?"

The muscles of his silk-clad arm tensed. "Vividly. You said no."

"Well," she said slowly. "I've changed my mind."

He darted a quick look at her. "You have?"

"Yes, with a few conditions."

She saw his jaw tighten.

"Don't worry, I'm not talking about marriage."

"What conditions, then?"

"As long as we're together, you must remain faithful to me only. No other women in your life."

"That's demanding."

"That's safe," she corrected. "I don't have any control over who you've been to bed with in the past but I'd like to reduce the risk in the present. I don't think it's asking too much in this day and age."

Pete was silent for a moment, then nodded. "Done. Although I would like to assure you that I've always been careful in the past. But, yes, I agree."

She'd been holding her breath as she waited for the answer. Now it had whooshed out. One down, one to go. "So far, our dates have involved going where *you* want to go. On occasion, I would like us to do what I want to do, which may sometimes include my daughter."

"I'm not a father substitute, Carly." His voice grew testy, distant. "I thought I'd explained that."

"You did. But I'm a mother first. If I'm supposed to take time and energy away from my family and give it to you, I need to know that occasionally you'll do the same for me and be an escort to me and Karen."

She could have reminded him that her daughter already had a loving father and didn't need a substitute. She could also have brought up the fact that Pete certainly needed Karen around far more than Karen needed Pete. But now wasn't the time.

"Do I get the right of veto?"

She nodded. "Of course. If you have something else you have to do, I'll understand. As long as you don't consistently ignore this side of the bargain."

"And you will want to be in my bed?" he persisted.

"Yes."

"Because that's where you want to be or because you think it's the right place to be?"

"Both." She smiled. "But especially the former."

His features lost their tension, resuming the gentle, teasing expression she loved so much. "What? An honest woman?"

"I always try to be, Pete. I'm asking you to be the same."

"When does this arrangement start?"

She feigned nonchalance. "Whenever."

"Today?"

Her heart skipped a beat. But there would be no time to take advantage of their new arrangement. The afternoon tea they were attending wouldn't be over until five. "I have to be at a baseball game by six this evening."

Pete steered the car onto an off-ramp and slipped onto the frontage road. He reached the top of the hill that bridged the freeway below and turned, retracing the road back home. At the same time, he punched a phone number into his car phone.

"What are you doing?"

"Making our apologies for not attending the tea."

"Why?"

"Because we're going back to my place. I'm not wasting a single moment of this afternoon with you at a tea party when I can have you in my arms."

Carly smiled. "Thank you for that," she murmured, leaning back in the leather seat and watching him drive toward home. She felt a coil of anticipation wind its way around her heart, but forced herself to relax. He didn't have to know just how much she wanted—no, needed—to be with him.

She listened to him make his excuses to the hostess while driving skillfully with one hand. When they reached the cutoff, he dropped the phone back in place and reached for her hand, placing it in his lap.

"Talk to me." His voice barked the words as if they were an order.

"I've almost finished grading papers," she said in a soft, teasing voice.

"That's not what I wanted to hear."

"Really?" She acted innocent, but the slanted look she gave him said more than she could convey in words. "What was it that you wanted me to say? Coach me and maybe I'll get it right the next time."

"Tell me you want me."

"I want you."

"Tell me why."

He wasn't going to settle for rote answers. She wasn't sure she could give him anything else.

"Tell me," he said again.

"I want a repeat of the same feelings we shared the other night."

She felt him stiffen in retreat. "I know what my feelings were, darlin'. But what were yours?"

Carly remembered after they'd made love, when he'd held her in his arms and she could breathe in the scent of him. It had felt so peaceful, so very wonderful. "Satisfaction." Simple, direct and to the point. Let him make of it what he wanted.

He stretched his fingers on the wheel. "That's it? Satisfaction?"

"Isn't that enough? What do you want me to say? What are you trying to get at?"

"I'm not husband material, Carly. Don't try to pressure me into that position."

"Heaven forbid," she stated dryly. "I am asking for you to treat me as an equal, however. If you expect me to give up time, then you have to expect me to demand communal time to spend with my daughter. Everything seeks its own equal, Pete. Women and relationships are no exception."

His gaze darted to her, then back to the road. "You're sure about this? You won't change your mind?"

She nodded. "I'm sure. The only rule that truly matters is that my daughter will always come first with me. Her life, her choices, her activities are all an integral part of my life. If you don't think you can manage that or fit us into your schedule, then please turn the car around and we'll head back to the tea party."

His rueful grin was slow in coming. "You think you've got me over a barrel, don't you?"

It was her turn to relax. The hard part was over. "No, but I am in a position to make you choose."

"Oh? In what way?"

"In two ways," she said leisurely. "First of all, you enjoy being with me or you wouldn't have continued to ask me out."

"What else?"

"We've both been victims of our own attraction for each other. It's about time we agreed to do something about it. At least until I find the person I want to spend the rest of my life with." It was a lie that rolled off her tongue as easily as a greased grape.

"Well, far be it from me to look a gift horse in the mouth." With a quick movement, Pete turned the car, then skimmed down the street toward his house. When he reached the driveway, he pulled smoothly onto the brick paving and punched a small button on the dash. Immediately the wrought-iron gates opened to allow him access to the private part of the drive.

Seeing Pete's beautiful yard would usually have interested her, but not this time. This time all her nerves anticipated his next move. Shortly she'd be in his bed and he'd be in her arms. All else was rendered insignificant.

When he opened her door and offered his hand, she eased out slowly without looking at him.

"My, you're calm, Carly." His voice was low and easy, his touch almost impersonal.

"So are you," she returned, following him up the path to the side door.

He let out a short laugh. "Not by a long shot."

His confession gave her courage. As he put the key in the lock, she leaned toward him. "No one would ever know," she whispered seductively in his ear.

Pete turned and swept her into his arms. "Don't play with my fire, Carly. You might get burned."

"I can take it. I'm tough."

He stared down at her so intensely that she wanted to look away from the heat. Instead, she stared back, returning look for look.

His tight hold slackened and his mouth, softened and the corners turning up. "I don't know about tough. But you're certainly direct."

"If you want less direct, I could play the coquette . . . for all of a minute or two," she challenged.

"Just for a minute? That's the best you can do?"

"It's as good as you playing the gentleman. You can't even bring me into the house without making a scene."

His grin was unrepentant. "Lady, I don't give a damn about who can see us doing what. This is my territory."

"And no one can see us from here, can they?" she guessed.

His grin widened. "Not unless they're peering through the side gate."

She thought of a thousand things to say, but didn't have a chance. Instead, Pete's mouth descended on hers. She parted her lips, letting a breath out slowly as she recognized she'd been waiting for this moment since they'd made love.

She wanted him to carry her away, to ravish her, to take the lead so she wouldn't have to admit to her own needs. But he refused. Instead, he played with her, teasing her mouth with his as he waited for her to show him she wanted more.

Carly wouldn't do it. She stood stock-still, waiting for the next step.

"Okay, lady. We're changing the rules and playing the game my way for a change," he muttered before swinging open the door and leading her to the Florida room at the back of the house. Once they were inside, he turned and pulled her into his arms for a kiss that was hot and hard.

She wrapped her arms around him and held on for dear life. His mouth explored hers, pulling emotions from deep within her as he took what he wanted. But as the kiss lengthened, his touch gentled, and his hands began to stroke her shoulders and arms. Then he slipped them around her waist and spread butterfly kisses across her eyes and cheekbones.

Her breath caught in her throat again.

"I want you, Carly."

"You've got me, Pete. Or would you rather I wrap myself up as a Christmas gift and sit under your tree?"

"I don't 'do' Christmas, you know that." He backed her against the couch. "Besides, you're just fine the way you are. In fact, the less wrapping the better."

Carly reached up and tugged at his tie. "I couldn't agree more."

He nudged her down onto the soft cushions of the curved couch. "We're here, now. Why not make use of the facilities available?"

Other than a soft moan, Carly never answered. She was too busy feeling Pete's hands and mouth on her body, caressing, soothing, heating everywhere. When she finally called out in ecstasy, Pete's low voice joined hers.

Afterward, they lay naked on the couch and watched the bright orange sun slowly set behind the pines. With his arms encircling her, she lay with her back curled snugly against him. Contentment flowed through every fiber of her being.

"You're full of surprises," Pete remarked lazily, pushing a strand of hair behind her ear.

"Thank you. I think."

"What's next on the agenda?"

"What do you mean?"

"I mean, what else do you have up your sleeve?"

"Not a thing."

"I'm surprised," he said dryly. "After this glorious afternoon, I thought you'd expect some kind of payback."

Anger welled in her. Did he think this was a bartering field?

"Actually, the payback, as you call it, is due next Saturday at one in the afternoon."

"So soon?" His surprise seemed genuine. But she was too angry to care.

"A baseball game at the Little League ball club by the YMCA. It'll take two hours."

"You're serious."

"You bet," she stated, standing and reaching for the clothing so negligently discarded earlier. "So be there."

She dressed with careful disregard of his stare. Suddenly she wasn't willing to compromise. If he couldn't accept her as she was, then he didn't deserve her at all. It didn't matter that she loved him, fool that she was. Nothing mattered except that he respect her for who she was. "Be there or lose me."

He stood and stretched. Naked in the golden dusk of late afternoon, he looked like an angry Greek god. "I'll be there," he said.

"HI, KIDS. THIS IS YOUR dad. I was just calling to see what you were up to. I miss you both. I'm looking forward to seeing you at Christmas. I send my love. Give each other a hug from me, will you?"

8

PETE SAT BUNDLED IN two sweaters and a Windbreaker, warmed by his clothes and the bright early-winter sun. From the bleachers, he and Carly watched a teenage pitcher wind up. Between them was Karen, yelling her heart out for the home team. Her dark auburn ponytail whipped this way and that as she studied the coach and players, then yelled the calls she thought were necessary to win. Though only seven years old, she was obviously satisfied with herself and happy in her life. The little girl showed a lot of character, but seemed to handle it well. So did her mother.

Since it was an afternoon game, the crowd consisted of parents and siblings of the players. Minutes before the game began, Pete had driven over from the house. Karen had been at viola practice, so she and Carly had met him at the ball club. Although Pete had spoken to Carly every day by phone, he hadn't had a chance to be alone with her since their Sunday-afternoon "tea." They were both pleased to see each other again, even if it wasn't in private.

He and Carly leaned against the steps behind them, enjoying Karen more the game. Every once in a while he would catch Carly looking at him as if he were a piece of rich, thick chocolate. His pulse quickened, his heart pounding with a deep hunger for her. Then she'd turn away and he would settle down a minute or so later, only to have his responses kick-start again at the next glance.

He must be insane. It was the only explanation for this craziness. He couldn't believe he was sitting on a hard wooden seat, watching a ball game he had no stake in, with a woman he wanted and a precocious child who was not his . . . and was enjoying the hell out of it!

He'd *better* be insane.

Just then he looked at Carly again, and found her eyes on him. The intimacy of her gaze made a slow heat flow through his body. He stretched his fingers a little farther along the bleacher back and touched her hand. Her look intensified, and so did his response.

Karen jumped up in aggravation and shouted, "Throw it, don't hatch it!" to an awkward teenage outfielder. The outfielder threw it toward the catcher, then waved his glove in Karen's direction. The little girl made sure the play was completed right, then plopped down with a sigh. "Tony's not gonna make it to the majors if he doesn't try harder."

"I take it Tony is the outfielder?" Pete looked to Carly for confirmation.

She shrugged, carefully hiding a small smile from her daughter. "I would guess."

"Sure he is, an' he's gonna be my coach next season," Karen continued explaining. "He's good but he's just not payin' attention."

"Put the ending on your words, honey," Carly reprimanded gently.

"Pay*ing*." Karen repeated the word absently, obviously used to her mother's admonitions. Then she asked, "How about a pizza after this, Mom?" Her gaze was still glued to the game. "It's the eighth inning and there's still plenty of light. I'll have lots of time to do my homework after we get home."

Carly glanced at Pete but didn't ask him to join them. Apparently she assumed he had other plans for the evening. He liked not being taken for granted—at least by the other women he dated. But not with Carly. He wanted her to tell him he could join them—*should* join them. He felt left out.

And he knew why. He was falling in love with Carly. Still, disastrous marriage, the loss of his children and his fear of being hurt again would always outweigh any impulse to get involved in a relationship.

Carly interrupted his thoughts when she answered her daughter. "I don't know why not, especially since your aunts are out this evening. Pizza it is, honey."

He wasn't going to ask. He refused to grovel. But his mouth formed the words anyway. "Am I allowed to tag along?"

Karen looked surprised. She glanced at her mom and back at Pete, then answered with a shrug, "Sure, Mr. Cade."

Carly looked just as surprised as her daughter. "I didn't know you ate anything that didn't have broccoli alongside it."

"Banquets and restaurants aren't the only place I eat," he murmured, tracing her hand with his finger again. "It just seems that way."

"Really? Somehow I can't imagine you feeling comfortable in a pizza parlor or hamburger joint."

"I took my kids often enough. But you've never asked me to either one of those places."

Her brows rose imperiously. "You've never offered to take me to one, either. It wasn't mentioned as an option on one of our dates."

Damn, he loved her quick mind. "What time are the aunts returning?"

Her eyes turned dark and he knew she was thinking about the same thing he was: how they could get together and make love tonight. Just the thought of having her in his arms made breathing difficult.

She turned away, a delightful peach flushing on her cheeks. "Around ten o'clock."

"Will you be taking a walk tonight?"

"Maybe."

"Let me know," he said casually. "I might walk with you."

Carly's only response was a slight nod.

They left immediately after the last inning, with Karen chattering all the way to the parking lot. When they reached Carly's car, Pete took the keys from her hand and opened the driver's door, then unlocked the other side so Karen could get in.

"Are you going to tell me where we're going?"

"You don't have to do this if you don't want—" She didn't complete the sentence because his finger touched her lips.

"I wouldn't have asked to tag along if I didn't want to spend more time with you."

The sunniness of her smile warmed his heart. "I'm glad."

AFTER SHE GAVE HIM directions, he followed her out of the parking lot and into traffic. He could see her talking to her daughter, laughing, smiling, listening as if the earth and the moon hung on the child's every word. A stab of regret hit him for all things that could never be.

He wondered what it would have been like still to have a family to go home to. But that would have meant still being married. Sleeping, eating, and dwelling with a woman he now knew he had never loved. It had been loneliness and habit that had kept him in the marriage, and it had taken anger—her anger—to force him out of it. He marveled at the time and energy he'd expended on a relationship that never had a chance.

But he'd loved the kids until he thought he'd be swallowed up in emotion every time he looked at them. Always wanting a big family, he'd never found a woman who wanted the same.

Until he met Carly.

His thoughts screamed the truth at him until his forehead popped out in sweat. No. He'd never get his hopes up only to get dumped again. And he was sure it would happen. Sooner or later she would see greener grass or find someone who was not quite so committed to his work. Then she'd cry "lonely" until he gave her a divorce and half his money.

No. He needed to keep Carly as a diversion only. What was wrong with him that he would even think about shooting himself in the foot again?

They reached the restaurant and he pulled up next to Carly's car. She smiled at him and he steeled himself against being drawn even closer.

Something in his expression must have warned her, for she stood very still while he walked up to her, her own smile slipping.

"Listen, I've remembered I need to make a few calls this evening before I leave for a gathering downtown," he said. "I don't really have time to stop right now. I hope you understand."

Karen stood between them, her eyes darting from one grown-up to another.

"I thought you wanted pizza," Carly said softly. He could see the hurt in her eyes, but he couldn't help himself. He had to get away while he could. The situation was just a little too threatening.

"I know, but . . ."

Her gaze continued to level him. He was torn between fleeing to escape from her and staying to be near her. Flight or fight.

"Let's go, then," he said. Although he didn't really mean to, he sounded as if he was being put-upon.

"Never mind." She spoke firmly. "We understand your busy schedule and that you need to be somewhere else."

"No, I have time. I just need to make a phone call," he lied.

Carly turned to Karen, who was still watching with complete interest. "Honey, go on in and see what video games they have. I'll be there in a minute."

She'd said, "I'll," which meant she was getting ready to give him the brush-off. His lips thinned. Like hell!

"You've done the baseball bit," she began as soon as Karen disappeared inside the building. "And I thank you for being such a good sport. I enjoyed it and so did Karen. But I certainly don't want you to be with us if you're not prepared to be positive about it."

She was dismissing him as if he didn't matter at all. His instinct was to retaliate. "Have you always been this blunt?"

"Yes."

"How many men has it scared away besides your husband?"

She tilted her head and looked him up and down. "Do you ever pick on someone your own size or only women you date?"

"I seem to recall your claiming that you're tough. What's the matter, can't take it?"

Suddenly Pete realized what he was doing—the same thing he'd always done when someone got too close. He was delivering barbs so no one could see his own vulnerabilites. For the first time he realized just what a cruel response it was. More than that, the thought of Carly walking away from him because of his insults forced him to realize just how much he wanted her in his life. "I'm sorry. I don't want to hurt you. It was just a reaction."

But the look in her eyes told him he'd already caused her pain. He needed to apologize. Again. "I'm sorry. I'm just not sure what to say or how to handle you most of the time, so I fight."

Carly gazed levelly at him, then let her breath out slowly. "This was supposed to be a day spent with my daughter. You were invited to come along, but don't think for a moment that I'm willing to forfeit this time with her. Although I love being with you, I'm not giving up her time for you."

He hesitated just a moment. "Do you like pepperoni?"

"I do. So does Karen." A small smile appeared on her face.

He grinned, praying she'd forgiven him. "Then let's eat, honey."

Karen had the time of her life. Pete promised an unending supply of quarters for the video games, giving her four quarters at a time. When Carly protested, he stated what he'd always said to his own kids: "Everyone needs to splurge once in a while. Besides, she's having a great time. What's wrong with that?"

"Plenty," Carly countered firmly. "She's a child, not something to be bought. Besides, if you give her this treat now, she won't think of my splurging as a treat later. Too much of a good thing is not wonderful when it comes to raising children."

"Unless you're talking about love."

She smiled, but she shook her head as if to chide him. "Love isn't a good or bad thing. It's as necessary as water and air."

"More homegrown philosophy?"

"Truth. And by the way, I don't charge for lectures."

"Much."

Her smile turned to pure, rich laughter. "Much," she admitted.

He watched her smile, mesmerized by the beauty of it. She was wonderful and sexy and utterly charming. Warning bells echoed in his head, but once more he ignored them. He'd only made the commitment for the evening. He was sticking by his decision. Anyway, he was having fun, wasn't he?

Karen hopped over to them on one foot, her ponytail bouncing in rhythm. Her eyes were alight with life. Pete saw the ghost of a young Carly and his heart warmed at the sight. The child had personality written all over her, just like her mama.

"You'll never guess! I was playing Ms. Packman when I heard somebody talking, and when I looked, there was my teacher!" Reaching for her mother's hand, she hopped on the other foot. "And she's my favorite person in the whole wide world! I mean, besides you an' Aunt Cora an' Aunt Nora. An', Shelby, who's my best friend in all the world. Oh, an' Daddy, of course." It all came out in a rush as the little girl continued to hop, using her mother's hand for support.

Carly glanced around before spotting the woman over in the corner with her own family. She glanced back at Pete. "Do you mind if I go over to speak to them? I'll only be a moment."

"Of course not."

He watched the gentle sway of Carly's hips as she walked across the room to the family perched around the heavy, wooden table. Karen danced by her mother's side, in some ways the image of her mother, except the younger version seemed to be in perpetual motion.

When he'd watched for three or four minutes, Carly turned and motioned him over. He rose reluctantly, realizing they had been asked to join the other family.

It felt strange to be considered part of a family again, but when he tested the thought, he found it comfortable. He slipped his arm around Carly's waist as he was introduced to the couple and their two children. Karen skipped over to the counter and informed the waiter where they were now sitting, and then returned to sit quietly beside her mother. Karen's wide-eyed look at her teacher said it all; she obviously idolized the woman.

When the pizzas were devoured, the last beer had been ordered and the children were off playing video games, Pete leaned back and talked leisurely about football with Dick, the teacher's husband. It was an easy conversation, one that allowed him to listen intermittently to Carly and her friend discuss the pros and cons of teaching at different levels.

Until he heard Carly's conversation, he'd never been aware of politics in the teaching profession. It dawned on him that he'd never asked about her work and its difficulties. He'd just assumed that she taught, then came home and paid attention to her family and him. She had an entire life of struggles to be dealt with every day, and he'd never bothered to ask or learn about them.

It certainly didn't make him feel very good about himself.

In the middle of his self-flagellation, he was also aware of Carly's every movement. When she tilted her head back, he wanted to kiss the long length of her exposed neck. When she strolled across the room to check on Karen and her friends, he mentally recorded all the sweet subtleties of her walk.

It was a challenge to sit next to her and pretend to be a longtime couple, as Karen's teacher and her husband seemed to think they were. Such couples didn't lust after each other the way he lusted after Carly.

But that was the only way it was difficult for him to fit back into being part of a couple. In fact he slipped into the role as if he'd been with Carly for a very long time.

He wondered what she was thinking. Had she planned for this to happen? He didn't think so, but he wasn't sure of anything. His manipulative ex-wife had made him wary.

Just then Carly looked over at him, her gaze as soft as a doe's and twice as shy. Like magic, all his inhibitions melted away, leaving the feeling that she had just touched his soul. Amazing.

He returned her look with one of his own, silently saying, "Your friends are nice, but I wish we were alone somewhere so I could make love to you."

Her response was just as potent. Her smile, slow in coming, warmed him to his heart's core.

Finally, dinner was over, the kids were tired and the adults were ready to end the day. Pete couldn't wait to get Carly alone, but he knew he had to bide his time. The two couples shook hands and exchanged banal pleasantries until they reached the doorway and stepped into the darkened parking lot. When the others left and Carly turned to him, he automatically opened his arms and enfolded her in a warm embrace. She stood inside the circle of his arms under the parking-lot lamplight, resting her head trustingly against his shoulder. A wave of protectiveness washed over him and he wanted to tighten his grasp and hold her so close she would never want to leave.

Karen stood beside them, her eyes as big and luminous as the light above. "Mom, are you okay?" Her voice, usually firm and confident, was soft and hesitant. It took Pete by surprise.

"I'm fine, honey," she reassured her daughter in low tones. Withdrawing her arms from Pete's waist, she reached for her daughter and gave her a hug. "I'm just tired."

The child buried her head in her mother's stomach. "I thought maybe the pizza made you sick," she said in a muffled voice.

Pete watched the picture the two of them made and realized he felt left out. More important, he found he wanted to be a part of it, part of a family again. Part of them.

Suddenly an emotional bucket of cold water washed over him. What in heaven's name was he thinking? Hadn't he promised himself that this would never happen again?

Clearing his throat, he got Carly's attention. "Will I see you later?"

She looked down at her daughter, then back up at him. Her green eyes were wide and deep. "Yes," she said simply.

Despite himself, he gave an inner sigh of relief. "I'll see you, then."

"Yes."

"What time?"

"I'll call," she promised.

"Around ten?"

"Okay," she said, nodding her head to confirm tonight's meeting. Placing a hand on Karen's shoulder, she turned toward her parking space.

It was time to retreat before he made a fool of himself. Without another word, he turned and left. He didn't look back. He just walked away and kicked himself for being all kinds of a fool. With his luck, it was a miracle she didn't think he was schizophrenic the way his emotions kept running hot and cold.

When he reached his Mercedes, he looked over the roof as Carly ushered her daughter into the passenger side, then slipped behind the steering wheel. Every motion was fluid and feminine. He'd dated a million women, but none had the grace, brain and sex appeal that Carly had.

So what was the matter? Why was he holding back?

He knew the answer. He wouldn't ruin a great relationship with marriage. Marriage changed attitudes. It made couples argue about stupid, silly things that never would have been a topic of conversation if they'd simply lived together. Marriage bred hate. He'd learned that lesson twice—once from his parents' marriage and once from his own. It didn't take a genius to know it would probably happen a third time.

Carly gave a little wave as she pulled out of the parking lot, and he raised a hand in response. But inside, he was confused. He wanted her in every way a man could want a woman, except for the one way he knew she needed to be wanted.

In marriage.

To Carly, marriage was salvation; something that represented love and commitment.

To Pete, it was everything he despised. But that didn't mean he didn't hurt or didn't have deep feelings of loneliness.

He would be with Carly for as long as he could. When she pushed for marriage—and he was sure it would happen sooner or later—he'd end the relationship. That way he was in control of the situation. In control of himself.

Meanwhile, Pete would take full advantage of every minute he had with her.

"WHAT THE HELL DO YOU mean, I can't visit at Christmas?" Pete demanded.

"Just calm down. After all, Peter, you're going to see them this summer."

"I want to see them at Christmas, too, and unless you've got a damn good excuse, I'll be there."

"Troy has a convention in Hawaii and the company is inviting families to attend, too. I'm taking the children with me."

"Fine." His voice was abrupt and direct. "I'll see them in Hawaii."

"I don't think so. Wait until summer, Peter, when they have nothing to look forward to. But to take them away from all the fun and excitement the other kids will be having isn't fair. The company is having all sorts of tours and experiences just for children."

"That's okay. They'll still want to spend some time with me."

"I don't think so, Peter. Be reasonable. Don't make them chose. You'd win, of course, but at what price? This opportunity may not ever come up again."

Damn her! He should have known she'd find a way to keep the children from him during the holiday. And she was right; the kids would choose him but their hearts wouldn't be in it.

"You win this time, Sandra. But the summer is mine."

"Yes, Peter. Of course."

Her voice was so demure, he wondered what else she had up her sleeve. Whatever it was, he wouldn't let it get in the way of their summer visit. No matter what.

9

CARLY WAITED IMPATIENTLY for Pete to open the door. She was half an hour later than she'd planned. After putting Karen to bed, she'd had to sit for a while with the aunts before she'd finally excused herself, hurried out of the house and cut through the woods to Pete's.

Would Pete think she was overanxious? It was too late to worry about that now. She was still trying to catch her breath when the back door swung open and he stood before her, a dark silhouette.

Gray cotton warm-up pants hung low on his hips and his bare chest emphasized the pure masculinity of him. Chilled breath caught in her throat as he slipped his hands into the elastic waistband of his pants and stood, daring her to enter. He could have been the devil incarnate, enticing her to hell, and she wouldn't have been able to run.

She swallowed hard, tilted her chin defiantly in the air and forced herself to speak. "If you're busy, I can come back another time."

He didn't move. She shifted on her feet uncertainly. "You're late."

His accusing tone got her hackles up. She stood just a little straighter. "I am not. I didn't state an exact time." She couldn't see his expression in the dark shadows.

"But if you feel that way, then I'll just leave the way I came."

"No, wait." He stopped her even before she turned. His voice softened, melting over her. "I'm acting like a jerk. It's just that I was waiting for you and when you didn't show up right away, I thought you might not come."

She relaxed just enough to be able to tease him. "Here I am. Do I get invited inside or did you ask me over to decorate the tree and hang mistletoe out here?"

"I don't celebrate Christmas, remember?" He stood aside, a sheepish grin on his face. "I'm sorry. I thought there was plenty of room for you to enter."

With as much panache as Carly could muster, she stepped inside. "There was. It was the invitation I was lacking." She walked through to the kitchen and waited for him to close the door before she spoke again. "You never told me why you don't celebrate Christmas."

"It's a lousy season. Except for when the kids were little, I never celebrated it." His voice grew distant. "Everyone pretends they're happy and have a family to be proud of. Suddenly at Christmastime there are no alcoholics, no drug addicts, no wife beaters or child abusers. Everyone denies all the bad stuff in the world and is happy with that pretense. The truth is, a whole lot of people are lonely, and this is the season that emphasizes that feeling the most."

Carly frowned, feeling indignant as well as sad. "Christmas is joyful and magical if you have friends with whom to share the wonders of the season."

Pete's cynical look told her he thought she was naive. "Did you know there are more deaths and suicides at this time of year than at any other?" He snorted derisively. "So much for the wonders of the season. It's pure commercialism. All of it."

It wasn't difficult to guess the source of his unhappiness. "Your children aren't coming for Christmas, are they?" Her voice was low and understanding.

"No." Pete snapped the door closed and gave a twist to the lock. "And since they're not here, I refuse to go through the motions of celebrating by putting up a tree and lights and all that other . . . stuff."

"You don't think your children sense that attitude? They need extra support and encouragement in their situation. Being shuffled back and forth across the continent can't be easy on them."

Pete frowned, then looked away with a shrug. "They don't seem to mind," he stated.

Even though the door was closed, she slipped her hands inside her jacket pockets and hugged herself. Now that they both stood in the kitchen, she could see his face clearly. His expression was strained and drawn, and his eyes were narrow slits aimed in her direction. Her heart went out to him. She wanted to comfort and love and help in some way, but she just didn't know how.

"Pete?"

He didn't answer. Instead, he walked toward her, not stopping until they were almost touching. For a split second, Carly thought that was as far as he would go.

She was wrong. He enfolded her in his arms as if she were the most precious package he'd ever held. He rested his head against hers and closed his eyes, taking a deep, sighing breath.

She felt the tension in his arms and back slowly begin to ease. He'd been as tense as a double-wound clock. Now she wanted to coax him into relaxing, to comfort him so that whatever was eating at him would go away. Using her hands, she began to silently soothe away his anxiety.

"It's okay," she whispered. "It's all right." It seemed like hours that they stood in their embrace, held together by their mutual need to balm his hurt. It was much later when his clasp finally loosened a little.

His sigh filled the room. "I did think you might have changed your mind."

It was just an excuse to talk. What was really on his mind was the subject he wouldn't discuss: his children.

"Is that why you're so tense?"

"No." He pulled away from her and she felt bereft of his touch. He rubbed the back of his neck as he walked across the kitchen, putting distance between them. "It's been a hell of a week."

It took all her patience not to ask the questions uppermost in her mind. Although she wanted to know why his children weren't coming to visit, she knew he would volunteer it if and when he was ready. All she could do was be there for him. "Is there anything I can do to help?"

"Yes." He spat the word out as if it tasted bad.

She waited for him to continue. When he didn't, she asked, "What is it?"

He turned and looked at her so intently, she could feel her body respond even before she heard his answer. "Make love to me."

Heat flushed her body in reaction to his words. Heat and a longing so intense it nearly pulled her across the floor and into his arms. Nearly. Instead, she forced herself to stand still. "Now? Just like that?"

His intense gaze never wavered. "Any time you want. Now. Later. I don't care, as long as you're in my arms making love."

"Is this some kind of test?"

"How?"

"You stand on that side of the room and taunt me with sexy talk to see what I'm going to do?"

"No. I'm just afraid to touch you without you knowing exactly what's going to happen. Because once I hold you, Carly, I'm not letting go until we're both satisfied."

Did that mean he needed release or that he needed release with *her*? She didn't know; and right this minute she decided she didn't care. He was with her now and that was all that mattered. "I don't see anything wrong with that plan," she finally said, and his eyes seemed to bore into her.

She held her breath as he slowly retraced his steps to her. For a moment her imagination took flight and she imagined him as a jungle cat seeking its prey. But when his arms wrapped around her in tender possession, she knew he needed to receive the affirmation of love as much as give it.

His mouth molded to hers exactly. His hard body pressed solidly against her pliant breasts. Tongue dueled with tongue for supremacy and she allowed him to win, this time. He led and she followed as they silently declared their building need for each other. When he finally pulled away, Carly felt dizzy. Afraid of losing her balance in the swirling world he'd created inside her head, Carly gripped his shoulders for support.

"Come," he said huskily. Holding her hands, he led her to the living area. The plush white couch wrapped invitingly around her form as he pressed her into the leather's softness. He lifted her sweater to nibble at her swelling breasts. A low moan rose from her throat, and she heard him echo that same sound as he went from breast to breast. She held his head, her trembling fingers running through his hair as his caresses carried her away.

In moments he'd undone her jeans and slipped off his sweatpants. "Tell me," he demanded, leaning over her and letting her see the intense need in his expression. "Tell me you want me."

She raised her arms to him, sensually and unconsciously imploring him to hold her close. "I want you. Now," she whispered. "Right now."

The softly spoken words were barely out before he pulled her into his arms and kissed her again. This time there was a demand, an impatience that didn't allow time to react. Willingly, she followed Pete's lead. His hands cupped her buttocks, bringing the heat of her to his own throbbing need. She felt his hardness and reveled in her ability to make him respond. He pulled her toward him and they sank deeper into the marshmallowy softness of the couch.

His kisses were mesmerizing, his touch nerve shattering, his body magical against hers. She loved him so much that tears slid down her cheeks. She opened her eyes and stared up at him.

"Am I hurting you?"

She smiled. "No." It was a lie. That he couldn't return her love caused enough pain to last her lifetime.

His thumb wiped away the salty liquid. "Then why the tears?"

Unable to explain the real reason, she shrugged. "I don't know. Happiness, I guess."

The tightness left his face and a deep sadness returned. He pulled back, and only Carly's hold on his waist kept him from standing.

"Don't go," she implored. "Stay with me awhile."

Slowly, he lowered his body to rest against hers, and she thrilled at the feel of his weight on her.

Unlike before, this time they made love slowly and sweetly, with mellow sounds and teasing touches. And when both had felt the release of sexual pleasure, they lay with arms and legs entwined and soft, satisfied sighs still lingering on their lips.

Carly lightly kissed the side of Pete's jaw, and he stared down at her, his gaze narrowing as he took in her expression. Pain flashed across his face and his eyes darkened to a stormy blue. "Don't, Carly."

She raised her brows questioningly.

"Don't fall in love with me. Both of us know that it won't work."

Anger filled her at being read so quickly and completely. Mostly she was angry with herself for showing it. She let out her frustration by hitting his shoulders to make him let her get up. "I'm sentimental, Pete, but I'm not insane."

Pete handed her the jeans she'd dropped on the floor earlier. "As long as you remember."

She stepped into them with staccato movements. "Don't flatter yourself. Love's got nothing to do with this relationship."

"Just wanted to be sure you understood," he muttered.

Carly glanced at her watch. "My, my, how time has flown. I've got to run. Busy day tomorrow," she said breezily. "I'll see you sometime next week?"

He nodded, still wary. "The benefit at the Kennedy Center is the second Saturday after Thanksgiving."

"Right." She walked toward the kitchen area. "See you then?"

"You're really leaving now?"

"Sure. We both relieved each other's tension," she said, wishing she was somewhere else so she could cry away the tears that drenched her soul. "It's time to get some sleep. I've got a full day tomorrow."

"Tomorrow is Sunday."

"I know. I have grading to finish that will take almost all day. And I promised Karen I'd spend an hour or so listening to her prepare for her viola competition next month. She has an opportunity to win a scholarship to Sweet Briar College next summer."

"Carly," Pete began, but she refused to listen.

"I'll be ready next Saturday. Meanwhile, if you have nothing else to do on Thanksgiving, you can always join us at the shelter on Twelfth Street. We're serving dinner."

"Carly," he tried again.

"Bye, see you later." She made a beeline for the back door and practically ran home through the crisp leaves.

The house was dark and silent, more quiet than outside, where chilling breezes rattled bare tree branches until they cried in eerie whispers.

Carly walked straight upstairs, checked on her sleeping daughter and then went to her study and stared out at the dark woods, her eyes focusing on the dim light at the back of Pete's house.

Here in her room, the tears began to fall in earnest, drowning out the fire of anger she felt for being stupid enough to fall in love with a man who wanted nothing to do with that emotion.

Her tears didn't stop until dawn broke.

THANKSGIVING DAY started early, but not in the same way it started in other households in the community. With two aunts dressed incongruously in jeans and flannel shirts in the back seat, Carly drove a sleepy

Karen to her father's home to celebrate Thanksgiving. Then she drove down to the shelter for the homeless.

Her first job of the day was to peel a hundred pounds of potatoes.

Her second job was to mash those potatoes once they were cooked.

"I thought institutional kitchens used instant mashed potatoes," she muttered as she mashed her third potful.

A regular worker heard her and laughed. "One of the farms in Georgia donated its bountiful crop of left-overs to us. The son of a gun didn't grow a crop of in-stant potatoes, so this is what we have to deal with."

Carly gave a grunt as she lifted the heavy metal pot. "At least I wasn't one of the poor people who broke their backs harvesting this crop."

"All done by machine. You're probably putting in the most amount of work to bring these potatoes to the ta-ble." The worker walked around her and added a bowl of peeled tomatoes to a vat of green beans. "Thanks."

"You're welcome," she said tiredly. But she couldn't complain too loudly. She had it easy compared to the people coming in to wait patiently for the food to be served. Carly glanced at the large school clock over the front door of the shelter. It was ten-thirty in the morn-ing. She and her aunts had been here for five hours. At eleven this morning, they would begin serving and wouldn't stop until four in the afternoon. The more she worked and the more tired she felt, the more grateful she was that she had a family, a job and the love of family and friends. It was threefold more than most of the waiting crowd had.

A day like this put everything in perspective for the coming season.

She continued to work at a steady clip, but her mind was never far from Pete.

He was having Thanksgiving dinner catered for some friends of his whose families were far away. Two members of the Canadian embassy, and several others would be there. Carly didn't know whom he'd asked to be his hostess. He'd invited Carly for the occasion, but she had reminded him of her promise to help her aunts. Pete hadn't seemed to mind her not being with him half as much as she minded being separated from him.

Damn him.

All of her attention was focused on the fact that they were going to the Kennedy Center this coming Saturday. She had already chosen a dress to wear—a rather simple but dangerous-looking full-length white knit, off-the-shoulder number that was both tasteful and sensual. She hoped.

It was to be like a farewell date for Carly. For her own sake, she had decided to stop seeing Pete. Their relationship was unfair to both her and her daughter.

Although he'd been great with her up to now, she knew Pete would never willingly become involved with her daughter, and that was deadly to an impressionable young girl. So, it was time to end their tentative alliance.

The bottom line was that she loved Pete far more than he cared for her. And that would never work.

Just as her mind was made up, the devil walked through the door.

Dressed in jeans and a chambray shirt, Pete entered the shelter, came directly to her and smiled. "Happy Thanksgiving."

"Happy Thanksgiving. What happened to your company?"

"They're right behind me. After we ate, I told them what you were doing and they decided they wanted to help, too."

She looked around to see what was the dirtiest job still open. Then she gave him a bright smile. "It's cleanup time, Pete. How are you at scrubbing pots?" she asked, almost sure he would back out.

"It's right up my alley, baby. Lead me to the kitchen."

She did as she was told. The rest of the day was spent supervising Pete and his friends as she continued her own work. Her volunteers had the kitchen organized in nothing flat and worked so hard they were able to keep up with the servers.

Every time she thought she had Pete figured out, he did something totally unexpected.

Damn the man, she thought. But the smile on her face belied her curse.

THE FIRST SATURDAY IN December, when the limo pulled up in her driveway, Carly was ready, with the help of the rest of the family. Her two aunts bustled around ensuring that Cora's ranch-mink jacket was drooping off the right spot on Carly's shoulders—casual but seductive. She walked out the door, with Karen and the aunts peering out at the car through the darkness.

Pete was still in the city. The driver was picking her up first, then she would take his evening clothes to his office. There, she would wait for him to dress and then they'd be on their way to the gala ball at the Kennedy Center.

Anyone in politics in the D.C. area would have killed for a chance to attend this particular ball. It was hard for Carly to believe she was going to be there.

The limo pulled away and she stared out the back window until she could no longer see Karen's dark hair and angel-white pajamas. She turned back to listen to the limo's superior sound system play the softly warbled notes of the Irish singer, Enya.

Her gaze drifted to the bar, then stopped. A crisp wine she liked had been chilled and opened and was ready for her to pour. Wasn't she living proof that Cinderella was alive and well and living in McLean, Virginia? But she was Cinderella without a Prince Charming, a little voice inside her said, and she realized how true that was.

When she reached Pete's town-house office in Georgetown, Carly found him stepping out of the shower and ready for the clothing she'd brought in the suitcase. He was dressed in less than fifteen minutes, chatting with her while sending a few orders via intercom to his secretary downstairs.

"Do you ever stop working?" she asked, sipping a glass of wine and watching him attach ruby studs to his tuxedo shirt.

"The moment I walk out the door."

"I doubt that. If that were the case, you'd never be at a party or banquet or dance."

"It's true. The socializing I do is for two reasons. One is for this year, and the other is for next year."

Her laughter spilled out. "Spoken like a true workaholic," she finally stated. "Castaways is lucky to have you campaigning for them."

"It's what I do best, but I need more donations to have enough funds for more technical training. Not everyone needs to go to college to earn good money, but everyone needs to have some kind of training. That's what I'm trying to get more of for our recipients next year." His smile had slowly faded into a frown. "There's so much loose money out there and yet people only go for causes that have charisma instead of honest need."

"You'll do well tonight," Carly prophesied. She didn't say so because she was trying to boost his ego; she stated it because she honestly believed that when Pete Cade made up his mind, he did what he set out to do.

"Thanks." He slipped into his jacket. "Ready?"

They drove to the center in companionable silence. Neither mentioned working together on Thanksgiving. It was something that credit was given for without words.

Knowing that liquor was plentiful inside, they both drank ice water while waiting for their limo's turn to pull up curbside directly in front of the entrance. Traffic was thick and the press even thicker, held back by ropes and kept in check by both uniformed and plainclothes guards and security people.

Once there, Pete stepped out and extended his hand, helping her to alight. Camera flashes popped, the crowd speculated and Pete smiled through it all as he led her toward the large doors to the party beyond.

Inside, they were escorted to their table where, after a brief apology, Pete made his way around the room, leaving her in the company of the others at the table.

She chatted, smiled, danced with strangers and listened to inane remarks on how beautiful the huge Christmas tree was. And the decorations—so Victorian. So white. So ivory. So today! She wasn't sure what that last remark meant, but it didn't matter.

Meanwhile, her heart knew exactly where Pete was at all times. Every time he talked to a beautiful woman, she knew. Every time he looked in her direction, she knew. Every time he moved toward her, she tensed. She was so aware of him that she felt as if she were split in two, one half talking and laughing to a roomful of strangers, the other half standing next to Pete.

There were times during the evening when she felt he purposely stayed away from her. She just wasn't sure what was the reasoning behind his actions.

One woman chose to follow him around the room. At first Carly thought it was by accident that the blonde was always in the same crowd as Pete. Slowly, however, she realized that it was intentional. Although he didn't seem to notice it particularly, Pete didn't seemed to mind, either. A shaft of jealousy speared through Carly, but she promised herself she'd ignore it—at least until later in the evening, when she was alone with Pete and could ask for an explanation.

The band was terrific, the guest singer one of the most popular in the country. The floor show was as good as anything in New York or Los Angeles or any-where in between. But Carly would have appreciated it more if her mind hadn't been so caught up in Pete.

By the end of the evening, she was wound as tightly as she could stand without breaking. Pete ordered the car brought around, then helped her with her jacket and escorted her to the front of the line, where their limo awaited.

"You had to pull some mighty tough strings to get the car this soon," she said, stifling a yawn.

"Not at all. People forget that the guys who park the cars and direct traffic are just kids. They make the de-cision on who goes where, and if you treat them like young adults, you get better service."

She leaned back in the seat and allowed the luxuri-ous intimacy of the limo help her relax for the first time that evening. She knew Pete was by her side and not across the crowded room. She knew the night was over and she didn't have to worry about the woman who followed him. She knew that Pete wasn't going to be .h that same woman tonight.

But would he be with her tomorrow night?

"Who was the beautiful blonde?" Her question was as subtle as a sledgehammer.

"Angela?" He untied his bow tie, then punched out the ruby stud at his throat and pocketed it. "She's a good friend."

Carly froze. "A lover?"

Pete looked surprised. "Now?"

Her heart sank and she wanted to kick herself for bringing the topic up to begin with. She was torturing herself with something that was out of her control. Normally she wasn't so self-destructive. "I guess that answers my question, doesn't it?"

"Only if it says that she was with me a long time ago, and I haven't dated her for quite a while."

Her lungs constricted. She felt as though a terrible burden were pressing heavily upon her. "Do you still date?"

He stared out the side window at the freeway lights beyond. "Occasionally, yes."

"We had an agreement."

"You said no one in my bed except you. I've kept to that, so far."

Those last two words jabbed at her chest like a dull sword. Carly winced but she didn't stop looking at him. "Was she supposed to be my replacement for tonight?"

"No." He turned and stared at her with eyes of stone. "You were hers."

She hadn't expected that. The words acted like a blade that slit her throat, leaving her powerless to say all the things she wanted to. Instead, she blinked, blinked again, then stared out the opposite window.

"Take me home first, please."

"You aren't spending the night?"

"No."

"Aren't you even staying for a little while?"

"No."

"Does this mean you've finally got mad enough at me to tell me to go to hell?"

She had promised herself that she would end it this evening. But she couldn't bear to put it into words. Not yet. "No."

His voice was strained. His gaze was riveted to the darkness outside, and she felt that same darkness in her soul. "Then what does it mean, Carly? That you'll keep taking abuse? That I'll keep dishing it out? Well, let me make it easy for you. It's over."

"Is that what you're doing? Trying to drive me away?"

Pete ran a hand through his hair. "Damn. I want you, but it will never go any further than it is now. I'm not prepared for more than an affair, Carly. I don't have any more emotions left in me to expend. The kids get them all and there're no more left." His hand fell to his side. "But I don't want to hurt you."

"What a kind, considerate man you are," she oozed, ignoring the pain of rejection that flared inside her like an out-of-control blaze. Everything—all hopes, all plans, all dreams—finally fell away. She closed her eyes to shield herself from the hurt, but it didn't help. This grief would never go away.

This would be the last time she could tell him the truth. He might as well hear it now, rather than never know how she felt. "I'm so impressed by your direct methods, I think I'll use them as a model." She took a deep breath. "In fact, I think I'll begin right now by telling you I love you."

She felt rather than saw Pete stiffen. His silence allowed her to continue.

"I love you so much that for just a little while, I almost excused your initial behavior toward my daughter. And that would have been a disaster, Pete, because she's mine, and I usually treat those close to me with much more respect."

Slowly he turned from the window to stare at her, his blue eyes looking dead already. A chill slid down her spine and she lifted her chin in lofty defiance. "I have an enormous amount of love to give, but we both know I'm a package deal, Pete. As much as I love you, I've never done anything to hurt myself. I refuse to begin now."

"So this is how it's going to end. Wouldn't you know it's in the middle of the Christmas season. I *knew* I hated the holidays for a good reason."

It was a statement but she treated it like a question. "I guess so. I was wondering how it would end, too. For a little while I deluded myself into believing that sooner or later you would take the chance and let yourself feel again. If you did that, then there was a possibility that you might fall in love with me, too. Then we would sail off into the sunset, a composite family that would love and be loved. And with a little work and a lot of understanding, we'd give all our kids the stability they would need in their youth so they could successfully launch their own lives."

"It's a pipe dream. Reality is a bundle of problems and they're all ugly."

Carly stared down at her hands entwined in her lap. They were almost as white as her dress. "If you believe it, then it's true. Most of my life I've made my own reality, Pete, and I'm not willing to be dictated to at this late date. I'll continue to look for my personal version of happiness and eventually I'll find someone to share it with. Someone who gives me as much love as I have to give."

"You're playing a fairy-tale game, Carly. Life doesn't work that way. All you'll wind up doing is hurting yourself and your child."

She nodded. "Maybe so, I don't know. But I do know that if I don't take a risk trying for the brass ring, I'll never have a chance at it. It certainly won't fall in my lap. Your problem is that you failed even before you began. You're unwilling to take the chance of loving for fear of getting hurt."

"More pop psychology?"

She refused to apologize. Instead, she looked him in the eye. "Yes."

"Sorry. But I've had the best psychiatrists sit at my table and they can't figure me out, so why should you be able to see everything so clearly?"

"Because they didn't love you. I do."

"I've heard that before."

She nodded. "I'm sure you have, but not from me. Others might love you in a tuxedo. I love you in sweats. Others love you when you're kind and generous. I love you all the time." Silence filled the car until she thought she could hear the crackle of the electricity between them.

The limousine pulled off the freeway and onto a side street. They were only a few blocks away from her home. Pete leaned forward, pushed a button and spoke quietly to the driver. "Miss Michaels will be going home first tonight, Jack."

The driver's gaze darted to the rearview mirror. "Yes, sir."

More silence. Carly sat quietly, dry-eyed and certain that she had done the right thing.

The car pulled into her driveway and slowed to a halt. Pete stared out his window, refusing to acknowledge her leaving the car. The driver got out and stood by her door but made no effort to open it. Apparently he knew they still had something to say.

The driver was right.

She'd decided she wouldn't leave without letting Pete know that he was loved.

"I'll miss you all the time. I'll hope that you'll change your mind and call me, even though I know better. But most of all—" she placed her hand on his black-clad arm "—I'll know that I told you I love you and that it was your decision to end this relationship."

He stared at the hand on his arm, then at her. "Is this where the tears begin?"

"No. This is where I tell you that I understand this isn't working. I'm crazy about a man who can't let go of the past, refuses to enjoy anything but the present and who has no future in my life. So, I guess this is the end of our, our..."

"Relationship?" he supplied, his cold tone freezing her all the way down to her toes.

"Business relationship," she corrected. "We can't call it anything more, can we?

"And now I'm the big bad wolf because I told you in advance that I wasn't interested in anything other than our present arrangement? Or should I be at fault because you didn't get me to change my mind and fall in love with you?"

Carly's shoulders slumped. "Neither. I'm not mad at you. It's not your fault I did what I did. But I want to ask one small favor of you."

"Ask away. I have the right to refuse."

She took a deep breath. "I'd appreciate it if you would treat me with the respect of a friend. If and when we meet, I would love to have a hug and hear how you're doing and what's going on in your life."

His brows rose in disbelief. "Are you a masochist?"

"No. But why harbor ill feelings? McLean has that small-town atmosphere. Look how often we've run into each other already. Let's leave this relationship with what we came in with—mutual respect and a fondness for each other."

He still didn't quite believe her. "You'll be okay with this?"

"As good as I'm going to be. I liked you before I loved you, Pete. Doesn't that count toward friendship?"

His finger came up and traced her full lips. "Damn, lady. If you don't beat all."

She smiled. "I know I do. You're the one who doesn't understand what you're giving up."

"Oh, yes, I do." There was such a depth of sadness in his voice. Her heart almost broke, hearing it.

Her hand tightened on the door handle. "Merry Christmas, darling, and a happy life."

The door opened.

"You're crazy." His voice was low and raspy and angry.

"Yes."

"I'll never love you."

"I guess not."

"Where's the anger? The resentment?" he demanded. "There was jealousy before, so there should be something left of that."

"That wasn't jealousy, that was pride. You were with me, so you needed to treat me with the respect due your escort."

Pete's groan was barely audible. "For that alone, you should hate me."

"I feel sorry for you," she countered. "With the high walls you've built up around you, you'll never know more than a surface kind of love. It's a sad and lonely way to spend the rest of your life."

"Don't bet on it, Carly. There are plenty of women out there who would enjoy such a relationship."

Carly leaned forward and placed a soft, gentle kiss on his cheek. Her eyes were bright with love. "Goodbye, Pete. I wish you better than that."

"Goodbye, Carly."

With the driver's help she got out of the car and walked up the steps to the door. The car door shut with a definitive click, but she didn't look back to see them drive off. Being brave was enough; she didn't need to rub salt in her wounds.

By the time she opened the door and stepped inside, she could hear the engine purring its way down the drive toward the street.

With a calm Carly didn't feel, she moved through the main floor, checking to make sure everything was all right. Then she walked up the stairs and approached her daughter's bed.

Karen was curled into a ball, her blanketed rump in the air.

Carly undressed, then slipped between the chilly sheets of her bed and lay motionless.

Still no tears.

Perhaps she was deluding herself. Perhaps she was afraid to look at the reality of her love. But it didn't matter. If Pete didn't want to be a part of her life, there was nothing she could do to bring him back.

So, with slow precision, she began building a brick wall around her heart, preserving her love for Pete inside. It was the only answer to her emotional survival.

"HI, KIDS, IT'S YOUR DAD. I know you're probably having a great time in Hawaii and are very busy, but I just wanted to let you know how much I love you. Call me when you get this message, okay? Bye, guys. Give each other a hug from me."

10

THE SHOPS IN AND AROUND Washington, D.C., were festively decorated for the Christmas season. The newspapers also reflected the season: along with all the ads growing bigger, bolder and brighter, the social columns ran longer, filled with parties from one end of the tristate area to the other.

Carly was aware of the gossip columns because her aunts kept her apprised of the various social events that listed "your gentleman friend, Peter Cade," as attending.

Rather than explain why she wasn't seeing him anymore, Carly told them that she was too busy with Karen's schedule and the last week of teaching to be their neighbor's escort.

That had truly been the case. She'd kept herself so busy, there was no chance to dwell on Pete—until nighttime. After Karen was in bed and the house was quiet, Carly would slip in a compact disk of sentimental songs and remember the good times she'd had with Pete. How his wry brand of humor had touched her funny bone. How his caring ways during their dates had made her feel so special. How the way he made love pushed every button in her heart and soul. But most of all, how they could discuss any topic, argue any cause, agree by degrees on any issue, and still consider themselves best friends.

When she wasn't sitting in the dark thinking about him, she was dreaming of him. In her sleep, he returned and told her just how wrong he'd been to leave her. He should have stayed and made the relationship work. He should have told her he loved her. He should have taken more time with Karen. He should have proposed....

It was usually at that time that she awoke, heated and agitated. She needed to make love. She needed Pete. But she would only admit that problem to herself in the dark of night. She couldn't afford the luxury of thinking about him by the light of day because then she'd surely go crazy.

For Karen's sake, she couldn't do that.

Whatever had scared Pete and made him afraid to love was his problem to deal with now. If he wanted to open up enough to have a loving relationship, he would find a way to do so. A small spark of hope buried deep inside her prayed that he would, but she really knew better. Carly had no choice in the matters of his heart.

All she could do was love him.

But a crazy, impulsive idea popped into her head. Despite his protests, she knew Christmas was a painful time for Pete. With a desire to remind him that Christmas wasn't such a bad season, she called an all-night florist and ordered a bright spring bouquet to be delivered to his house in the morning.

He had probably given enough of them in his life, but she'd bet he hadn't received too many.

She hoped he liked them. . . .

NAKED, PETE WANDERED through his dark house, pretending he wasn't drawn to the back windows every five minutes to check the night view. But he knew what he was looking for—Carly taking a walk in the woods late at night to sit on "their" bench.

If he did see her out there, he wasn't sure if he had enough willpower to stay away. God! He missed her.

She'd been on his mind every waking hour since last week, when he'd finally driven her away with his uncaring attitude. He'd done it on purpose, even as he'd secretly hoped she wouldn't leave. And he still hoped. It was this damn season, he told himself. When it was over, he'd lighten up.

"Nothing like shooting yourself in the foot, Cade," he muttered to the warm, quiet house. "And if that wasn't enough, you punished yourself even more by shooting your other foot."

But the house didn't care. It didn't answer back. And as big and spacious as it was, it was filled to overflowing with the ghost of Carly. Everywhere he turned there was a memory of Carly, laughing, resting, reading, talking, and even crying. There were memories of making love to her in various rooms of the house.

Unfair! his mind cried, but he knew better. Those memories were his punishment for hurting her so badly. He could have done it differently, but for the life of him he didn't know how. He'd hacked at her feelings with dull blades of words until he was sure anything she felt for him was dead.

She'd just turned the other cheek.

This afternoon the florist had delivered a huge bouquet of spring flowers along with a note. The note was classic.

> Thank you for all the good times we shared. I appreciate them. I hope these help you stay cheerful through the season.
>
>   Love, Carly

Since he'd received them he hadn't thought of anything but Carly.

And with every thought he became angrier. How dare she invade his thoughts! How dare she take over his every waking moment! And all with a cheap trick. Hell, he sent flowers to every Susie and Jane he knew, usually to get what he wanted. But not once, ever, had a woman sent him flowers.

Until Carly.

The grandfather clock in his study pealed the hour, one dong at a time. It was ten o'clock. Walking to the phone, he dialed her number.

When Pete heard her voice, he almost lost his. He cleared his throat. "I got your flowers today. Thank you."

"You're welcome." Her voice was warm and sweet and wonderful.

"You shouldn't have spent that much."

"It's the least I could do to let you know I'm thankful for the three beautiful dresses in my closet as well as the good times you gave me."

"It was nothing."

"Are you all right?" Her voice flowed like liquid honey over his raw nerves. Her honest concern soothed the hurt and anger he'd felt all evening.

"I'm fine."

"Pete, don't let the Christmas season get you down."

"I won't. It's just a lousy time, that's all."

"Then change it. Go find what it is you need to make you happy during this season."

"I can't," he answered curtly. "Anyway, thanks again."

"You're welcome. Again."

"Goodbye."

He hung up the phone and closed his eyes tightly. She was so sweet, so full of care and concern. And dignity. No request to get back together, no hints of picking up where they left off. Just a hand extended in friendship. It messed up his mind and body.

Pete continued his prowling through the house until the wee hours of the morning, when he fell asleep on the couch with an afghan thrown over him. When he awoke the next morning, there was someone banging on his door. He cursed, wrapped the Afghan around his middle and went to answer it.

"Yes?" he barked.

A young man stood in the doorway wearing a uniform with a patch that said We Deliver Anything. "Sweet delivery, sir," he stammered, looking Pete up and down. He held out a package like a peace offering.

"I didn't order anything."

"I know. Someone ordered it for you." The kid backed away quickly, edging toward a rainbow-painted van.

Pete patted his pocket, then realized he didn't have pants on. "Wait, I'll have to find my wallet."

"No problem. I'll catch you next time, sir."

He was in the van before Pete could close the front door.

He went into the living room, allowing the afghan to drop as he walked. The package had all his attention. Stepping around the oak cocktail table dominated by Carly's flowers, he plopped down on the sofa, tore off the small envelope and read it.

He should have known.

This is for your sweet tooth late at night. Have a wonderful and very Merry Christmas.

                                                              Carly

"Damn her," he muttered. He'd thought of nothing all night except Carly Michaels, and by this morning he believed he'd finally begun to understand her behavior. Pete had decided that she'd sent the flowers to let him know everything was fine between them. That she had no other motive.

Now he wasn't sure.

Was she trying to woo him in a way he just wasn't familiar with? Was she trying to buy him back?

Since no one was around·but him, he spoke aloud: "With flowers and candy that you could buy with pocket change, Cade? Get real!"

No, deep down he knew better. Carly had always been thoughtful and considerate of his feelings—far more than he had been of hers. This was just one more thing that underlined that fact.

He went to the phone and dialed her number. When the answering machine picked up and the message finished, he spoke.

"I got the candy and I want to thank you. But the flowers were enough. Really. Thanks again, friend," he said to remind himself more than Carly just what their relationship was.

The call was just what he needed to do. Now his conscience was clear; he'd done the right thing for Carly.

He opened the box, chose a caramel and bit into the candy. It was chewy and the taste was sweet, but it didn't stop the loneliness he felt.

He told himself that he needed his children, but his heart told him that he also needed a woman's love.

Bull.

WHEN PETE DROVE INTO his driveway the next day, he was physically and emotionally spent. He'd had little sleep the night before and had put in a hectic day.

The tiredness that comes with not sleeping for two nights had finally caught up with him. He barely kept his eyes open as he drove into the four-car garage. He dragged his feet as he walked through the enclosed breezeway into the kitchen.

With an arm that felt as if he'd been lifting hundred-pound weights, he threw his overcoat and suit jacket over the kitchen chair. The maid had cleaned thoroughly and the house was immaculate, thank goodness.

He tugged at his tie until it hung down the front of his shirt, made his way to the living-room wet bar and poured a splash of brandy into a crystal snifter. After swirling it around to give it a little warmth, he sipped at the golden liquid.

He could fix something to eat.

He could start a fire.

He could call the kids again and see if they were home yet. When he'd called this morning, they were still asleep. By the time they were awake and eating breakfast, he was in a meeting that lasted over four hours.

Damn, he missed them. He had a sneaking suspicion that if he prodded them, his daughter and stepson would say they missed him too.

But the bottom line was that they wouldn't be here this Christmas. And Pete could barely afford to spend a day or two there. His schedule had become overrun with meetings. He tried to delegate some of his workload, but it had been a part of his life for so long that he couldn't imagine not dealing with the responsibilities himself.

He swirled his brandy as he headed up the stairs. Exhaustion was quickly overwhelming him. Just as he reached the top, the back doorbell rang. Cursing under his breath, he debated whether or not to answer. Duty won and he finally returned downstairs and to the kitchen, grumbling all the way.

When he opened the door, a bundled-up Karen stood there, her red-mittened hands holding out a large envelope. "Hi, Mr. Cade. Mom said I was to give this to you and tell you that you really need to smile." She cocked her stockinged head and peered up at him. "Are you still sad?"

Pete stared into the large, childish eyes and wondered how to cope with a little girl's questions. Honestly, an inner voice told him, and he followed that advice. "Yes, I guess I am."

"Why?"

"Because it's Christmas and I won't be spending this time with my family like you will be with yours."

"That's awful," Karen admitted solemnly. "I'd be sad, too, if I couldn't see my mom and dad."

"I know."

"Where're your mom and dad?"

"They died," he answered.

"Oh, that's awful." The little girl shook her head. "It's a wonder you're not crying alla time."

For the first time all day, he felt a smile tug at his mouth. "It is a wonder, isn't it?"

She nodded, her brow furrowing. "Are you all alone? You don't have a mom or kids to play with?"

"I have children, but they're living far away now."

"Oh," she said, as if finally understanding something. "Is that why you're always so grouchy?"

"Is that what you think I am?"

She grinned. "Kinda. Mostly about me, though. I bet when you look at me, you see your own kids and you get sad."

How did this child get so smart? The smile he'd been holding back completely disappeared. "That's right. I love them."

Her head bobbed up and down. "I know, 'cause my dad says the same thing when he can't see me."

"How do you feel when he can't see you?"

"I miss him, but then I know I'm gonna see him again soon, and that we'll have fun together." She stared up at him. "He loves me with all his heart. He always tells me that."

"I see. You're very grown-up about your parents' divorce, aren't you?"

Karen held her mittened hands in front of her and took a deep breath. "Yes. You see my mom and dad 'splained to me how much they love me even though they were gonna live in two different places. An' sure enough, they do."

"You're very lucky."

Her piquant face showed her surprise. "I am?"

At that moment, he realized just what Carly had been saying about her daughter. She was secure in her feelings for her parents because they had chosen to overlook all the petty issues in their relationship and work toward making their child stable. It was something he and Sandra hadn't done . . .

"That you have parents who love you," he said.

"And my cat, Hank Aaron," Karen reminded him. She might be wise but she was also a child. "He loves me, too."

"I'm sure he does." His voice was soft, his mouth turning up in a smile despite his sadness.

"Well, I gotta go. Mom said to say Merry Chrispness. You're gonna like it."

"Like what?"

"Your present." The little girl turned around and headed down the path back to her house. Her breath came out in small puffs that she watched as she walked.

"Where is it?" he called after her.

"Right there, silly." She laughed, pointing to a spot outside, just under his breakfast-nook window.

Pete stared after her. He stared so hard his eyes glazed over and protective tears formed. As she disappeared down the path, he heard her singing a song about three wise men.

He returned to the kitchen and shut the door behind him. Then, with even steps, he went over to the breakfast-nook and looked out the window for Carly's surprise. A large wooden box stretched the width of the ceiling-to-floor plate glass. Brimming with brilliant scarlet geraniums, it created a patch of brightness against the bare garden beyond.

He realized he was still clutching the envelope Karen had brought to him. With stiff fingers, he tore it open and read the paper.

Just because we weren't right for each other doesn't mean that we were wrong. I think of you often, but only in good ways, wishing you the happiness you seem to want but are afraid to reach out and grab for yourself. Perhaps, if just a few things change to make you happier in your personal life, you'll make the rest of those changes yourself. So, to help, I'm sending spring flowers your way to remind you that the next season is one of beauty and growth. I wish you all the happiness you can handle.

Love, Carly

For the first time since his divorce, Pete sat down and cried.

CARLY PULLED UP TO the self-serve tank at the gas station and stepped out. It was another harsh winter day in a week that seemed filled with them. She had to step gingerly on the icy drive as she swiped her credit card through the machine and began the process of filling her tank.

"What the hell are you doing outside?" Pete's gruff voice questioned.

She turned with a ready smile, her heartbeat increasing just because he was near. He was sitting in his car at the service tank across the aisle. "Hi. How are you?"

"Fine, but you didn't answer my question. Why aren't you in your car letting the attendant fill your gas tank?"

She laughed. "Spoken like a man who never heard the word *budget*."

"This is freezing weather, you're wearing dress boots, and you think it's smart budgeting?" He opened his door and stepped out. He was in a full-length cashmere coat. It was almost as gorgeous as he was. Underneath she glimpsed a dark blue suit that had to be Armani. It would have paid her fuel bill for three or four years.

"That's right," she said as he approached. Her fingers were getting colder by the second and she readjusted the pump handle in her hand. "It's over twenty-three cents a gallon cheaper. What do *you* call it?"

He took the handle out of her hands. "I call it silly. Get back in the car and stay warm. I'll do this."

Because her teeth were chattering, she did as she was told. Once in the driver's seat, she turned and watched out the window as he filled up her car.

When the attendant walked up to him and he paid for his own car being filled, Carly couldn't help the laughter that bubbled up.

Pete put the hose back on its perch and walked to her window, his frown deepening. "What's so funny?"

"You," she said, laughing. "Your car is in the full-service lane and an attendant is filling your Mercedes, while you're filling up my little economy car. I think I'll write a letter to the company, telling them how much I enjoyed their service."

His grin was reluctant, then rueful. "Okay, so it's a little weird," he finally granted.

Carly barely contained her chuckles. "You could say so," she managed. "But I'm not complaining, you understand."

"I understand." He rested his hand on the door and leaned down, his face so close to hers that she could have leaned forward and kissed his mouth. "By the way, thank you for all the gifts. I don't deserve them."

"Of course you do," she stated firmly. Her insides might be jelly but she wouldn't let him know how she felt: he might fear that she was being possessive and then stay away. Then they'd never have a chance to grow closer. "And you're quite welcome."

"Is everything going all right?"

Her smile brightened. "Everything's going very well, thank you. School was out last Monday. I'm almost through with my shopping and it's Christmas. What more could I ask for?"

"Riches. Prince Charming." He glanced up at the dark, snow-laden clouds. "A house in the Caribbean."

"I have all the riches I need. My Prince Charming has decided I'm not his princess." When he opened his mouth to protest, she placed her warm hand over his cold one. "And that's okay, because I enjoyed it so much while we were together." She smiled. "But a house in the Caribbean isn't a bad idea. I might work on that one."

His blue gaze was intense. "You're a special lady, Carly."

"Thank you for noticing."

He stared another moment, then suddenly stood straight. His hand patted the door. "I've got to go. Take care."

"You too," she said. A minute later he'd driven off, but she knew she would hear from him soon....

THE NEXT AFTERNOON Pete was in a hurry. He'd foolishly decided to return home before attending a dinner party in Georgetown and traffic had tied him up. He didn't know why he'd decided to stop off at home; he just wanted to touch base. He drove into the garage, then walked through the kitchen and began shedding his clothes on the way up the stairs.

Then he spotted the door. All the delivery people knew to place package tags on his beveled glass door. There was a tag and, upon closer inspection, he saw a bundle hidden under his doormat.

She'd done it again. He knew it. Part of him wanted to ignore the package and pretend he hadn't seen it. But another part brimmed over with curiosity. What gift had she sent this time?

He stepped back down the stairs, his tie in his hand. He opened the door and reached for the slim package. It came from a well-known store at the mall.

Shutting the icy chill out, he ripped open the package, then stared incredulously at the fabric in his hand. It was an expensive pair of men's silk boxer shorts. The design was what got him. It was a bow-legged Santa throwing a kiss. Around the waistband were the words Happy Holidays.

He should have known that yesterday's gift wasn't the end.

Attached to the plastic wrapping was an envelope with a letter. Filled with frustration and anticipation, he quickly read the note.

If Santa can be happy during this busy season—and heaven knows he's got plenty of work to do—then so can you. Wear these in good health and with happy smiles. I blow you a kiss of friendship.

He looked from the letter to the shorts and back again.

Then his laughter burst loose, filling the silent house with a joyous sound.

As he went up the stairs, he realized he just had to wear them under his tuxedo tonight. No one would ever expect a cool businessman like him to wear loud, ridiculous underwear like this. He loved the dichotomy, even if he would be the only one aware of it.

With this gift, Carly's mission had been accomplished. For a little while he felt like a happy man....

THE NEXT EVENING he drove home in silence. No radio, no motivational or novel tapes, just the dulled noise of traffic as he sped along. Worn-out from paperwork, politics and a pending litigation, he was staying in tonight.

Some big-shot attorney in Tulsa, Oklahoma, was threatening to sue the corporation because the shelter was keeping his wife out of his reach. It didn't matter that she and their two children had hidden from him in shelters twice before and he had found and beaten them within an inch of their lives each time. It didn't matter that the poor woman didn't have a dime to show for herself after living for twelve years with a wealthy man. The attorney needed his punching bag and would do just about anything to get it.

Pete's job was to restrain the jerk from suing, while keeping the woman mentally stable enough not to run back to him to keep peace. Pete had spoken to her several times on the phone, and she had finally begun to relax.

Financial status didn't matter when it came to domestic problems. Men like this jerk were in every social stratum. There were bullies of every type, rich and poor.

As he pulled into the driveway, he glanced at his front door and realized he was unconsciously bracing himself for one of Carly's gifts. He didn't want any more. It was too easy to fall into the trap of believing life was good and sweet and kind. Everyone wanted that fairy tale, but life wasn't like that. Through his years of work with the shelters, he'd learned the hard way that real life was strife and hatred and boiling anger. Carly was too naive and he was too cynical for them ever to agree.

Real life was his millionaire father beating the hell out of him with a Hermès belt. Real life was his mother silently standing by, or crying like a wounded animal while she was beaten. Real life was hiding in the back seat of the Rolls-Royce convertible parked in their four-car garage, hoping his father would pass out from the liquor before his rage got out of control.

It wasn't until much later, after his father's fatal heart attack, that his mother turned her life around. She began working untiringly in a local shelter—so hard she was ready to drop at the end of each day. It was as if she couldn't do enough to remove the guilt of her passive existence in the past.

But Pete thought he could. At one time he'd thought he could change the world. He'd even thought that having a family and raising them properly, with love instead of anger, with hugs instead of hits, would make a difference.

He was wrong. Instead, he'd lost the very people he loved. And now, it seemed, he'd lost the capacity to love.

So he worked like his mother had before him. Tirelessly. And he kept his love to himself. That way, he wouldn't get hurt. Neither would anyone else.

Slamming the car door, he walked into the house. Then he saw it.

Outside, propped upon the railing of the walkway was a large bag with a cluster of yellow ribbons streaming down the sides. The top of the bag had been split open a few inches, and several birds were busy pecking at its contents. Peeping out of the front corner was the expected envelope.

After staring at it for several minutes, he turned and continued through the house. He maintained his usual routine of loosening his tie and getting his brandy, then went upstairs to change into a comfortable warm-up suit. He would ease into his library chair and work another couple of hours.

Later, around dusk, he cooked a steak on his indoor grill, lightly fried potatoes and onions, and made a salad. Then, sitting at his breakfast nook, he ate while staring outside. His yard lights softly illuminated the area surrounding the house highlighting the bright red geraniums and the winter birds chirping and pecking at the yellow-ribboned bag of seed.

Finally he couldn't stand it anymore. With angry strides he stalked outside and grabbed the envelope that had called to him from the moment he'd spied it. Once back inside, he sat down and opened it.

Not all birds fly south in winter. Perhaps as you watch them, you'll realize they're optimistic enough to believe their friends will be returning soon. Meanwhile, let them remind you that spring is around the corner. Where spring is, there is summer, and your children aren't far behind for their visit over the holidays.

A lump formed in his throat. He swallowed hard a few times, telling himself that it was just the steak. But he knew better.

The image that haunted him the most was of the night she told him she loved him. They'd sat in the dark limo outside her front porch. She'd very carefully told him off and done it in a way that was classy and honest.

But did she really see him as so depressed that he couldn't get through the season? Could she possibly believe he was so lonely he needed birds for company? The answer was a resounding *yes*.

Well, it didn't matter. He'd ignore her presents and sooner or later, she'd stop sending them. Then he could ignore her opinion, too.

That was it. That was the answer. Pay no attention to her and she'd leave him the hell alone.

"HEY, KIDS, IT'S YOUR dad. I haven't heard from either of you in a while. How about dropping whatever you're doing and giving me a call, okay? I could stand a little love coming this way. Soon. I miss you both so very much. I also happen to love you both. Talk to you later. Bye."

"By the way, I cleared a day to visit you before you leave for Hawaii. I can't get any more time off, but you're not getting away with being out of school and not seeing me. Love you. Bye."

11

PETE WAS WRONG. Although he hadn't bothered to call and thank Carly for her last two gifts, it didn't seem to stop her. The next day he found a wrinkled brown paper bag on his back porch. Inside was a mediocre bottle of champagne, two vanilla candles, a container of children's bubble bath and a romance novel on whose cover was a half-clothed woman swooning in the arms of a Neanderthal. However, the story took place in his favorite historical period, the Italian Renaissance, and Carly had once mentioned that women's romance novels were as stringently researched as those in the general fiction category. With idle curiosity, he began reading the book while doing exactly what she'd told him to do in her note: sit in a bubble bath with lighted candles. The story turned out to be pretty good, and the bath was as therapeutic as a spa.

It was a new experience for him and he wouldn't have wanted anyone to catch him doing it, but he was more relaxed than he'd been in a long while. However, more than once, he found himself thinking of having Carly join him. He shoved that thought aside as quickly as it came. He was crazy to be thinking about a woman who was harassing him with gifts.

He laughed sourly. Who the hell was he kidding? She wasn't *harassing* him. But her offerings were becoming a burden. He knew she was on a limited budget and couldn't really afford them. He wanted to make her stop, but aside from being rude, he couldn't think how to do it.

He continued to ignore them.

THE NEXT MORNING Pete flew to Los Angeles. He took Cynthia and Ian to a mall for some shopping and then to the Hard Rock Café for dinner, where they ate hamburgers and discussed all the rock-and-roll artists' wild and weird guitars hanging on the walls. The kids were happy to see him but filled with stories of a life and friends he knew nothing about. This emphasized even more the growing gap between him and his children.

But one thing reassured him that he hadn't really lost them to another man, and that was the love they expressed for him. Cynthia was growing into a young lady, but when it came to her dad, she was still the little girl who wanted to hold his hand.

And Ian definitely wanted to be "cool," but didn't mind admitting how much he still loved putting together his model airplanes. It gave Pete a great sense of satisfaction that Sandra's new husband couldn't get the hang of painting the models; nor could he distinguish a fighter plane from a bomber. It was petty, he knew, but that knowledge acted like a balm for his bruised ego.

When Pete returned home the next day, there was nothing waiting for him. He felt relieved. She'd finally got the message. No more gifts.

But just to make sure he was right, Pete checked the front-door area. Nothing.

He checked under the mat. Nothing.

Then he sorted through the mail his maid had left on the hall table. A small package sat there, bearing Carly's return address.

With a sigh of mingled regret and relief, he opened it. A small paperback sat in his palm. He read the title aloud: *"Looking For Love in All the Right Places."* It was written by a noted psychologist whose main thrust was working on loving relationships within a family and finding that elusive inner happiness.

The note was short and sweet.

It's just as important to learn how to receive as it is to give. I hope you receive this in the spirit in which it's given. Happy Holidays.

His hands tightened, almost crushing the book. She knew what buttons to push, damn her. As much as he protested against the thought, his younger years had been filled with the idea of finding just the right woman for him, having a dozen children and living happily ever after. He was going to be the best parent, always there when his children needed him or his advice. He was going to be the best husband, helping with all those chores that kept a household running. He was going to be his wife's best friend, making sure she would never want for a confidant or lover. He would give his all.

This small paperback brought all those old dreams back as well as all the sadness of knowing it would never be. And looking at the book, he felt the regrets he'd felt back then, when he still clung naively to his stupid, marital dreams.

Like a zombie, he went into the living room and reached for the portable phone. His fingers jabbed at the numbers, then he waited impatiently for her to answer. But when she did, he almost lost his voice.

"No more, Carly."

"What's wrong, Pete?" Instead of being sarcastic, her tone was filled with concern. "Are you all right?"

"Stop the gifts."

"It's Christmas, Pete. I hope you'll find the season a little more bearable this way."

"No. Don't give me anything more. You can't afford it, and neither can I."

The silence on the line said more than either of them could put into words. "Use them in good health, if not with someone special, then by yourself," she finally said softly. "Be good to yourself. Merry Christmas." Then Carly gently replaced the receiver.

Pete never made it to his pile of paperwork that evening. Instead, he drank down three scotch-and-waters and muttered every trite expression he could think of that pertained to women. But when night came, he stretched out on the couch and began thumbing through the stupid book, reading the entire first half.

By the time he went to bed, he knew the answer. Finding love was something that everyone seemed to want, but it was never easy. According to the statistics in that book, half the people never found a partner they could commit to for life because they were never willing to take a chance on loving without being loved in return.

It was going to be a rough night for him.

THE FOLLOWING NIGHT Pete slept at his office. It had been an emotionally rough week and he deserved a little uninterrupted sleep. His feelings could do with a rest.

But the next day a snowstorm was coming in from the west, so it wasn't a hard decision to go home. He was sick of work, sick of politics, and definitely sick of his social calendar. He wanted to hide away and not talk to a living soul for a long time. He wanted to eat and sleep and curse when he wanted to. If the storm lasted three or four days, it would be all right with him.

As he left the garage and entered the breezeway, he noticed Karen stomping her way back toward her house. Before he could stop to think out his decision, he called to her.

"Karen!"

Wrapped up like baked potato in winter clothing, she turned around tentatively. In her mittened hands she held a tinfoil bundle. "I'm supposed to give you this, but you weren't home."

"I just drove up," he said, opening the door to the breezeway and letting her in.

They walked to the kitchen door, then she stopped and carefully wiped her feet before stepping onto the tile floor.

"I didn't know if you were coming, so I didn't want to leave this in case those nasty mice found it."

Pete knew he wasn't following something. "Mice?"

"That nasty Tommy Richmond has a hundred of them. He thinks that just 'cause they're white, they're okay to scare people with."

Pete knew the Richmonds lived just a few houses down from her aunts' home. "If you pet them, he'd stop teasing you."

The little girl looked up at him with surprise in her green eyes—green eyes that looked just like her mother's. "That's what my dad says."

Pete tried hard not to grin. "Your dad and I know what makes little boys tick. What does your mother say?"

Karen carefully placed her bundle on the table. "Mom says his dad should teach him some manners and his mom should tell him how to treat a young lady."

"That sounds about right."

"But I won't let Mom talk to him yet, cause I want to play T-ball next year and his dad is the coach."

"Tommy won't keep you from the team, Karen."

"He sure would," she stated defiantly. "He sure would."

"When do they sign up?"

"Right before Easter, Mom says. I can't wait."

"Do you think you'll be good?"

"Oh, yes." Her head bobbed rapidly up and down. "I'll be terrific!"

He couldn't help the chuckle that burst out. Nothing like knowing your talents. At least she didn't take offense.

"I'll go now, but Mom says Merry Christmas," she said, pronouncing the last word carefully. "Me, too, Mr. Cade. It must be awful to be an orphan. There's nobody to buy you gifts and you're too old for Santa to give you more than one present."

"It's a shame, isn't it?"

"I know. I'm sorry." She was so earnest. Karen's eyes watered as if she were going to cry, and it hit Pete in his heart like nothing else had. "I told God to be extra good to you."

He reached out and patted her shoulder, comforting her. Her childlike concern was earnest and sweet. Like her mother's. "I'm okay. I promise."

She blinked several times. "Are you sure?"

"I'm sure."

"Okay, then. I'll tell Mom to stop worrying about you, too, Mr. Cade."

"Thank you," he said softly. "And you can call me Pete." But by the time the last word was out, Karen was gone from the kitchen. With a wave, she was out the breezeway and on her way home.

"See you!" she called over her shoulder as she disappeared into the fat flakes that forewarned of the storm. "On the first day of Christmas, my true love gave to me." Her young voice carried across the snow.

Pete glanced up at the sky and decided to stock up on wood for the fireplace. He made several trips to the woodpile, bringing logs into the breezeway so he wouldn't have far to go for a fire later that evening.

Suddenly Karen's song echoed in his mind. He stopped. Of course! Carly was giving him her personal rendition of "The Twelve Days of Christmas"! It would all end on—he counted the gifts given so far—on Christmas Eve.

He walked inside and unwrapped the foil package the little girl had delivered. Piled high inside were rich Toll House cookies and fresh, warm, chocolate brownies. The note on top read: "Take with a glass of milk and call us Christmas Morning."

Still holding the note, he bit into a cookie. Delicious. Damn. Taking her suggestion, he poured himself a glass of milk and sat down at the table to begin the systematic devouring of a plate of goodies.

Always being out and entertaining in the best restaurants never gave him the thrill home cooking did. This was just a small example of what he missed.

She was right. Milk was perfect with this treat. Still clenching her note in his hand, Pete ate the whole plateful.

WHEN HE AWOKE THE NEXT morning, the countryside was a winter wonderland. The tree limbs were decorated with crystal icicles and the bushes were draped in a mantle of snow. Everywhere was the peaceful serenity of a place untouched by man's footsteps.

As he padded into the breakfast area for a cup of coffee, he saw a note attached to the window. It didn't take a moment to realize that Carly had made another trip. He stared at it for a long time before stepping outside in the freezing weather to pull it off.

Below the note was a shallow basket filled with pinecones. A rose, green and cream plaid ribbon decorated the handle. The note read, "Get rid of your frustrations the easy way. Chuck one of these into the fireplace and watch beautiful colors spring to life. Enjoy, and Merry Christmas."

Was she shoving this whole season down his throat until he hated everything about it?

Stupid! his mind cried out. *She's trying to make you appreciate the wonder of Christmas.*

But I don't want to know the wonderful things about Christmas if I can't have my children with me! he fumed back.

Your children are in California. Nothing will change that. Does that mean you should be miserable the rest of your life?

Yes, dammit!

Then you can stay miserable!

Fine!

His anger got him through the rest of the day. The storm wasn't as bad as the weather forecasters had feared and the state did its job of clearing the streets quickly which enabled him to attend an open house an old friend was having that afternoon. Their home was brightly decorated with hundreds of garlands, wreaths, angels, and two Christmas trees. Ornaments, candles and arrangements proclaiming the season were everywhere. His friend, a government official, had a marriage and family Pete envied. It was evident that his friend had a near-perfect home life.

Pamela, the svelte blonde he occasionally dated, was there. She was as nice, sweet, attentive and sexy as ever. He was cold, disgruntled and on edge, but he invited her over to his house the following night anyway. There were only a few nights left of this season; he might as well be occupied through them.

Even in this crowd, it was the loneliest evening he'd ever spent.

THE NEXT MORNING, as he stepped out the door to his car, he found a package hanging like an ornament from his breezeway door. He yanked it down and stared at it. It was a compact disk of all the classic Christmas songs by great old artists, including Mel Tormé singing "The Christmas Song."

He slapped it against his leg and stared out at the backyard. The bare trees made it possible to see Carly's house. He spied the park bench that stood about halfway, partially hidden by an evergreen bush. Memories flooded him, especially of the first time he saw her—in a mound of leaves, looking like the angel she was.

Why couldn't they have gone on the way they were? Why did Carly have to want more from their relationship? Why wasn't what he offered enough for her?

He felt an immense pain well up inside him. It was too hurtful to describe, too intense to brush off, too complicated to understand.

Forcing himself to go about his normal business, he got into his car and drove to work. Just out of curiosity, though, he played the CD in his car.

He'd get through this season if it was the last thing he did. And, feeling the way he did right now, it damn well might be.

He couldn't stand much more....

CARLY BUNDLED KAREN UP and followed her aunts out the door.

The freezing night air enveloped them as they joined the church choir group and marched to the first house to sing Christmas carols. She knew they would eventually wind up in front of Pete's home, and she wasn't looking forward to it.

At the beginning of the gift-giving frenzy, she'd only wanted to let him know she loved him and that it was still all right for them to be friends. She'd wanted to enjoy any part of him he might want to share. After all, they lived just a little ways apart, belonged to the same church, knew the same neighbors and even bought gas at the same service station. They were bound to meet each other again.

Besides, it saddened her that he felt so much resentment for a season that was meant to be joyous and celebratory. Giving love to others without recompense was what the season was about, and she wanted him to realize and enjoy that fact.

But of all the gifts she could have given him, she would have wanted to be able to arrange for his children to be here. She understood his loneliness. If Ken had taken Karen away from her, she would have withered and died inside. Holidays were when she needed her daughter's presence the most. Karen was the reason for the festivities.

Right after the divorce, Karen had been her incentive for getting out of bed in the morning. She'd been the purpose behind a smile during the evening meal and the laughter as they watched some silly sitcom together.

But now, the last two days before Christmas, with only two more gifts to deliver to Pete, she felt the futility of it all. He didn't want her gifts, he didn't want her. In fact, she probably did him more harm than good.

"Oh little town of Bethlehem..." they began singing, and Carly joined in, opening the songbook at the proper place.

Just as they ended the carol, a light dusting of snow filled the sky and dropped on their heads like diamonds from the heavens.

By the time an hour had passed and they were ringing Pete's doorbell, the fairy dusting had turned to fat flakes of snow that landed and stuck on everything.

When his door opened Carly caught her breath. He stood in the large entryway, illuminated by the golden light overhead, a smile slashing dimples in his cheeks as he listened to them break into another Christmas song.

Her heart pounded in her chest as she went forward and very carefully set a small bottle of homemade liquor on the top step. Her gaze locked with his and for just a moment she couldn't move, couldn't think, couldn't breathe. He'd caught her with her love for him shining in her eyes and glowing on her face. He'd caught her as surely as the moon rose and the tides ebbed.

His own look was just as intense and just as desperate. His gaze spoke silently of the love they might have shared—the feelings of contentment, of fulfilled dreams, of living happily ever after.

Then a figure joined his in the doorway and he seemed to mentally disconnect himself, stepping back and becoming an impersonal neighbor again. As the carol continued, Carly stared at the blonde woman at Pete's side. She was the same one he'd been with when she'd had her blind date with Terrence. They were together again. If she thought she'd felt pain before, she was wrong. Anguish seared through her like a red-hot knife, severing nerve ends.

From the beginning, Carly had tried to squelch any hopes, but apparently she'd harbored some she didn't know she had. There was no other explanation for the hurt she felt now. She had brought this punishment on herself.

She barely finished the song.

Luckily it was time for Karen to get home to bed. As she and Karen cut between houses and through the woods, she tried to hide the tears that were running down her cheeks.

Karen rattled on about the things happening in her life and Carly tried to pay attention, but all thoughts were focused on the scene at Pete's door. She'd read his brief look all wrong. She'd interpreted what she'd wanted to see instead of the reality of the situation.

It was good that she'd seen him with Pamela, she told herself. It was the one thing that could make her understand there would be no going back. He didn't want her love. The message had been harshly delivered, but at least he was honest about it. It was over. He'd told her that before. And she had agreed.

But it hurt so much!

"Tommy's dad said I could be the first girl on their T-ball team, Mom," Karen said, as she tried to skip through thick snow. "Isn't that neat? He said that Pete spoke to him about sponsoring the team, too, and that we'd all get new uniforms!"

Carly stopped and stared down at her daughter. Her voice could barely function but she managed. "What did you say?"

Karen told her mother again. Then she pulled Carly toward the house. "I'm cold, Mommy. Let's get some hot chocolate. You promised."

"Yes, baby," she responded absently, her mind whirling. "Why would Pete do something like that?"

"I dunno."

"You should call him Mr. Cade, honey. It's not polite to call a grown-up by his first name."

"I know, but he tole me to!" the little girl stated with exasperation.

"When?"

"When I took him the brownies."

Why would he try to become familiar with a little girl who reminded him of everything he'd lost? Carly couldn't come up with an answer. It was just something else he'd done that she couldn't find a reason for.

Karen was finished with that topic and moved on to what Santa was bringing her for Christmas. Her list was never ending.

Carly got her daughter ready for bed and then talked to the aunts for a little while when they returned from the church. By ten that night she was dressed in an old Bugs Bunny T-shirt and standing at her darkened bedroom window. The clear but chilly night scene looked like something on a postcard.

Somewhere out there, Pete was probably in bed with a blonde who wouldn't demand love. Who wouldn't ask for her child to be loved. Who wouldn't . . .

Carly turned away from the window and slipped into bed. It didn't matter who he was with. It wasn't Pamela's fault Pete didn't love Carly. It wasn't even Carly's fault. Or Pete's. It just *was*.

But that reasoning didn't stop the overwhelming sorrow she felt deep in her soul, or the tears that wet her pillow.

CHRISTMAS EVE WAS AS beautiful a day as could have been ordered. The snow was crisp and clean, the air clear, the sun shining brightly.

Carly woke and went through the motions of the day for her daughter's sake. If anyone noticed her occasionally less-than-enthusiastic behavior or her subdued smiles, nothing was said. For that she was grateful.

But all day a single question nagged at her mind, and it concerned Pete. Should she give him the last gift? She'd worked on it for days. It was meant to be the culmination of her efforts to help him accept Christmas. For all she knew, though, the blond woman could have decorated the interior of his house from top to bottom, making her small effort a joke.

Or...

She made up her mind. She got dressed for cold weather, then stepped into the garage. In the corner was a live three-foot spruce tree in a nursery container she'd painted in bright Christmas colors. Tiny white lights and bows of rose, cream and forest green decorated the branches. At the top was a plastic star covered in tin foil. Carly, her aunts and Karen had all signed their first names on it with indelible ink. On the back was even Hank Aaron's paw print.

Carly tried not to think about what she was doing as she picked up the tree, placed it in Karen's old wagon and walked around the block to Pete's front door. She gathered her nerve and rang his bell, then waited.

It was with a sense of relief mixed with disappointment that she realized he wasn't home. Carefully, she picked up the plant and carried it close to an electrical outlet on the porch. After setting it down and plugging it in, she walked away. Even if he'd found someone who made him happy, the feelings she wished to express with this gesture were still there.

As she turned the corner, she glanced back. It was a good, if sad, feeling to realize the twelve days were over and she was done. If she'd done a good job, Pete might forever remember this holiday and think more kindly of Christmas in the future. If not, she'd lost a few dollars and a little sleep over the planning, but none of the satisfaction of doing something for another.

PETE ARRIVED HOME LATE that night. On the porch, glowing with tiny white lights, was a little Christmas tree. It was live and sweet, and made him realize just how stupid a man he could be.

He sat on the front steps and stared through the darkness at the tree for a long time. He couldn't believe that he'd ever thought Carly'd had had intentions in giving these gifts. The tree wasn't a threat to him. All it did was sit there and light up the night.

How old did he have to be before he quit being an ass and began to live life the way it was meant to be lived, with love and laughter instead of sadness and hardship?

Suddenly Pete knew what he had to do if he was ever going to have the happiness he'd dreamed of all his life.

And he'd damn well better do it now, before it was too late.

CHRISTMAS MORNING dawned as beautifully as the day before. Carly awoke resigned to having lost Pete's love.

She might never know the true reasons behind his behavior. But accepting that their relationship was over was also a lightening of that burden. Besides, he deserved credit for enriching her life and giving her the greatest gift of all—the ability to look at herself as a desirable, feminine woman again. That was something she could treasure for the rest of her life.

These thoughts eased the sadness that had taken root deep in her heart.

Carly marveled at the energy displayed by her family as they opened their packages. The aunts seemed to get as much joy from watching as they must have had as children. Even Carly got caught up in the excitement.

An early-afternoon Christmas dinner was easier to manage than Carly had expected. The aunts had always had friends over, and they didn't change their routine this year. Although usually a little scatter-brained, they knew exactly what to do and did it. Two hired women came in to help in the kitchen.

Dinner went off without a hitch. The company, several friends whose families were far away, shared the buffet-style meal. Afterward, everyone sat around and enjoyed dessert and conversation before leaving for home.

The aunts helped the hired girls clean up, shooing Carly away. So she took advantage of the lull, and went into the living area to play a board game with Karen.

Later that evening, Aunt Nora came downstairs from a quick nap, still wearing her dressy brown caftan with a festive holiday scarf tied around her neck. She stuck her head in the doorway. "Dear, did you ever hear from Peter about coming to dinner?"

"No, Aunt Nora." In one of the notes, she'd asked him to call on Christmas morning, but he hadn't. A vision of the blonde flickered through her mind, bringing her pain to the forefront again. "I think he accepted another invitation."

"Such a shame that young man couldn't have come. Well," she said, tightening her scarf around her neck, "it's his loss, as they say. Cora cooked the best turkey in the South."

"I wish Pete had come, too, Mom. I could have said thank-you for getting my team new uniforms," Karen said.

"Mr. Cade," Carly corrected absently, as she noticed a car pull up in their driveway.

"He said I should call him Pete."

Carly stood and walked toward the window to get a closer view. "Very well," Carly said, not really listening. She moved from the window to the front door. It was Pete's car that was parked in the driveway, but a man dressed like Santa was walking up to the door. Could it really be . . . ? her mind cried out. The pleasures of heaven and the pains of hell couldn't stop her from answering his knock.

"I didn't think you would come," she said, standing in the doorway.

"Merry Christmas to you, too," he called in a booming voice, stepping inside and brushing off a few snowflakes. "I hope I'm not too late for gift-giving."

"Nope," Karen volunteered. "I knew you'd be here. You liked Mom's brownies too much."

"How do you know?" Santa asked.

"Because you were smelling them as I left."

Pete chucked her under the chin and continued. "Well, is everyone ready for their presents?"

Completely mystified, Carly led the way back into the living area and sat down. It hurt almost as much as it felt wonderful to see him. She didn't understand what he was doing here.

He saw the question in her eyes and chose to ignore it. "Where are your aunts, little Karen?"

"Here we are, Santa." Cora and Nora appeared and played along as if this happened all the time. "We were wondering if you were going to drop by."

Carly watched in silence as he produced two gifts from his bag and handed them to the older women. With oohs and ahs, they unwrapped them and exclaimed over the beauty of their new pearl-and-gold brooches.

Next came Karen's gift. She ripped off the paper and squealed in delight. It was a baseball and glove and a certificate from Nolan Ryan's coach saying he would spend an hour giving her instructions in a batting cage. Nothing could calm her down. She jumped up and down, laughed, kissed Santa and squealed some more.

As the aunts guided Karen away and left the two alone in the room, Carly turned and confronted him.

"That's a very expensive present."

"Yes, it is. But Hal's a friend of mine and he thought it would be fun to coach a little girl for a change. It's only for an hour."

The doorbell rang and Karen went screaming to it. "Daddy! Daddy!" she shouted when she opened the door. "Guess what? I'm gonna get batting lessons from the same man who taught Nolan Ryan! Isn't that just great? Isn't it?"

Ken and his very pregnant wife walked in the door. He picked up his daughter. "Whoa, little one. Explain it to me, but first let me say Merry Christmas to everyone. Okay?" He gave each of the aunts a peck on the cheek and then entered the living room. His gaze lit on Santa first, but he came over to Carly and gave her a kiss on the cheek. "Merry Christmas, Carly. I hope you're having a good one."

She smiled, her attention still on Pete. "It's lovely. How about you two?"

Ken's wife smiled and patted her stomach. "Wonderful. It's a quiet day for a change."

"Hard to believe any child of Ken's could be still for a moment," Carly teased. The two women had worked out their differences and established a comfortable relationship. It made for an odd peace, but peace just the same.

The pregnant woman laughed. "I know what you mean."

"Don't gang up on me, now," Ken warned, then held out his hand to Santa. "Ken Michaels," he said.

"Santa Claus," Pete replied.

Ken's brows rose, but he let it go. "Well, are we going to be offered a little of Aunt Cora's special pecan pie before we leave?"

Aunt Cora's face turned pink with pleasure as she led them toward the kitchen.

Once more, Pete and Carly were alone.

Carly sat down as Pete reached for his beard and hat, pulled them off and dropped them to the floor. He sat beside her.

She stared at him in wonder. He was so handsome that her heart raced just from looking at him. And he was here, in her home on Christmas Day, dressed in a Santa costume.

Carly couldn't help asking the question uppermost on her mind. "What is it? Why are you here?"

"I've had thirteen days to do nothing but think about us."

Carly remained silent, waiting for the punch line she knew would come. He didn't want to see her again. He thought her gifts were juvenile.

"I should have known you'd be hard to get out of my head." His words were softened by a smile. "Until you came along, I had pretty solid opinions about life. From my work with the shelters and personal experience. I viewed relationships as being one long struggle. It never dawned on me that there was an easier way to deal with life—that is, until you came along."

"An easier way?"

"I know it sounds stupid coming from a man who's supposed to have some kind of intelligence, but I didn't understand that relationships weren't always a battle, and that ending a relationship didn't mean you had to become enemies. You showed me that you could continue to work together without hurting others."

"I don't follow," she admitted, still confused.

"I guess I'm saying that you have a unique relationship with your ex-husband and, at first, I didn't believe it was possible. But now I know that whatever you worked out with him has had a wonderful, stabilizing effect on your child."

"We both wanted that," she said.

"Well, thanks to your example, I called my ex-wife last night and we had a long talk."

Carly's heart pounded. So that was it. He was thanking her for his ability to finally open up a little. Well, it wasn't love but it was the next best thing—she'd given him some peace. "Is she sending the kids for Christmas?"

"No, but at least she's willing to talk about next year." He sighed. "This attitude is still new to me. It will take a little time to get over some of the bad stuff."

"I know. But you'll be happier later," she said softly. She wished she could hold him for a moment and let him know just how loved he was. But that wasn't in the cards. Not now.

"Carly—" he leaned forward and took both her hands in his "—I know you have every right to be angry with me. And I know that if you let me, someday I'll explain about my parents and how I came to be like this, but this isn't the time. You already know that losing the closeness with my kids has hurt me more than I can say. They weren't only the object of my love, they taught me how to love. When I lost them, the pain was so great, I promised never to let myself open up to anything that could do that to me again. Then you came along."

Carly's heart began soaring out of control, but she was still afraid to hope. Could this be a thank-you and goodbye? It was certainly possible.

"Carly," Pete began again.

She couldn't stand it. Placing her fingers over his mouth, she interrupted. "Hush, Pete. I'm glad you're grateful. I'm glad I've helped influence your life for the good. But please, no more hurt."

His eyes widened. "Hurt? How?"

Once more she was blunt and to the point. "You know how. Don't give hope when what you mean is thanks."

"Do you love me?" he asked, his voice rasping with emotion.

"Yes."

"Will you marry me?"

Every muscle in her body froze. "What?" she finally managed.

"Will you marry me?" He smiled. "I love you with all my heart. Besides, I'm tired of running from happiness, honey. And you're happiness. You make me smile in the morning, smile in the afternoon, smile at night. You are kind and giving, and I'm a dirty rotten scoundrel for wanting to tie you up and keep you for myself, but that's what I want."

"I *am* a package deal, Pete," she said carefully. She wouldn't risk doing anything that might harm her child. "Karen has to be just as welcome in this marriage as I am."

His smile was tender. "I understand that, honey, from my point of view as a father as well as yours as a mother. And the fact is that I really like your daughter. She and I get along pretty well, and I think the rest will come with time. What I was thinking is that we could gauge how well my relationship with her goes until Valentine's Day. If it's okay, then we can be married on that day."

Carly opened her mouth once or twice, then snapped it closed.

Pete got up and pulled her with him until she stood in his embrace. His blue-eyed gaze was so intense she could feel the heat of it warm her insides. "Please say yes."

"Yes," she whispered. "Yes," she said. "Yes!" she cried.

Then Pete's mouth moved over hers and stole her breath away.

It might have been her twelve gifts that showed him how to love her. But it was his one gift of sharing that love that would carry them through the years.

"Hi, honey. Listen, I want you and your brother to get ready for a surprise. Remember Carly, the woman I told you about? And remember I told you we might get married? Well, the wedding's going to be on Valentine's Day. Kids, I can't wait for you to meet her. Carly's so special that she tells me she won't marry me unless you guys like her, too. I'm confident that you will. But just in case, I'm sending a private jet to pick you up so you'll be here before the wedding. I've already checked it out with your mom and she's agreed to the trip. Oh, and you get to meet Carly's daughter, Karen. She's just a little younger than you are, Cynthia. And she always wanted a big sister and brother, especially one who plays professional baseball! Anyway, I love you and miss you so much that I want to see you before you come here. I'll be out there next week. I'll bring pictures and lots of hugs, so you'd better be ready for me.

"Oh, and tell your mom and stepfather hello for me. I hope all is well.

"Love you!"

SECRET FANTASIES

Do you have a secret fantasy?

Chris Nicholson does. A widow, she'd like to find the perfect daddy for her little girl. She'd also like to find the perfect lover for herself and explore her deepest desires. But is all this too much to ask of Greg? Find out in #522 *LOVE GAME* (January 1995) by bestselling author Mallory Rush.

Everybody has a secret fantasy. And you'll find them all in Temptation's exciting new yearlong miniseries, **Secret Fantasies**. Beginning January 1995, one book each month focuses on the hero or heroine's innermost romantic fantasies....

HARLEQUIN®
Temptation

...not the same old story

SF-G

On the most romantic day of the year, capture the thrill of falling in love all over again—with

Harlequin's

Valentine
Bachelors

They're three sexy and *very single* men who run very special personal ads to find the women of their fantasies by Valentine's Day. These exciting, passion-filled stories are written by bestselling Harlequin authors.

Your Heart's Desire by Elise Title
Mr. Romance by Pamela Bauer
Sleepless in St. Louis by Tiffany White

Be sure not to miss Harlequin's Valentine Bachelors, available in February wherever Harlequin books are sold.

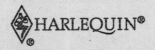

AMERICAN ◆ ROMANCE®

This holiday, join four hunky heroes under the mistletoe for

Christmas Kisses

Cuddle under a fluffy quilt, with a cup of hot chocolate and these romances sure to warm you up:

#561 HE'S A REBEL (also a Studs title)
Linda Randall Wisdom

#562 THE BABY AND THE BODYGUARD
Jule McBride

#563 THE GIFT-WRAPPED GROOM
M.J. Rodgers

#564 A TIMELESS CHRISTMAS
Pat Chandler

Celebrate the season with all four holiday books sealed with a Christmas kiss—coming to you in December, only from Harlequin American Romance!

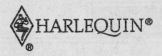 **HARLEQUIN®**

 *Weddings, Inc.*

The proprietors of Weddings, Inc. hope you
have enjoyed visiting Eternity, Massachusetts.
And if you missed any of the exciting Weddings,
Inc. titles, here is your opportunity to complete
your collection:

Harlequin Superromance	#598	*Wedding Invitation* by Marisa Carroll	$3.50 U.S. ☐ $3.99 CAN. ☐
Harlequin Romance	#3319	*Expectations* by Shannon Waverly	$2.99 U.S. ☐ $3.50 CAN. ☐
Harlequin Temptation	#502	*Wedding Song* by Vicki Lewis Thompson	$2.99 U.S. ☐ $3.50 CAN. ☐
Harlequin American Romance	#549	*The Wedding Gamble* by Muriel Jensen	$3.50 U.S. ☐ $3.99 CAN. ☐
Harlequin Presents	#1692	*The Vengeful Groom* by Sara Wood	$2.99 U.S. ☐ $3.50 CAN. ☐
Harlequin Intrigue	#298	*Edge of Eternity* by Jasmine Cresswell	$2.99 U.S. ☐ $3.50 CAN. ☐
Harlequin Historical	#248	*Vows* by Margaret Moore	$3.99 U.S. ☐ $4.50 CAN. ☐

HARLEQUIN BOOKS...
NOT THE SAME OLD STORY

TOTAL AMOUNT	$
POSTAGE & HANDLING	$
($1.00 for one book, 50¢ for each additional)	
APPLICABLE TAXES*	$ _____
TOTAL PAYABLE	$ _____
(check or money order—please do not send cash)	

To order, complete this form and send it, along with a check or money order for the
total above, payable to Harlequin Books, to: **In the U.S.:** 3010 Walden Avenue,
P.O. Box 9047, Buffalo, NY 14269-9047; **In Canada:** P.O. Box 613, Fort Erie, Ontario,
L2A 5X3.

Name: _____

Address: _____ City: _____

State/Prov.: _____ Zip/Postal Code: _____

*New York residents remit applicable sales taxes.
Canadian residents remit applicable GST and provincial taxes.

WED-F

CHRISTMAS STALKINGS

All wrapped up in spine-tingling packages, here are three books guaranteed to chill your spine...and warm your hearts this holiday season!

#302 THE KID WHO STOLE CHRISTMAS
Linda Stevens

#303 I'LL BE HOME FOR CHRISTMAS
Dawn Stewardson

#304 BEARING GIFTS
Aimée Thurlo

This December, fill your stockings with the "Christmas Stalkings"—for the best in romantic suspense. Only from

HARLEQUIN®

I N T R I G U E®

If you enjoyed this book by

RITA CLAY ESTRADA

Here's your chance to order more stories by one of
Harlequin's favorite authors:

Harlequin Temptation®

#25461	TWICE LOVED	$2.99	☐
#25574	THE COLONEL'S DAUGHTER	$2.99	☐
#25600	FORMS OF LOVE	$2.99 U.S.	☐
		$3.50 CAN.	☐

Harlequin® Promotional Titles

#83238	TO HAVE AND TO HOLD	$4.99	☐
	(short-story collection also featuring		
	Debbie Macomber, Sandra James, Barbara Bretton)		
	(limited quantities available on certain titles)		

TOTAL AMOUNT	$
POSTAGE & HANDLING	$
($1.00 for one book, 50¢ for each additional)	
APPLICABLE TAXES*	$_____
TOTAL PAYABLE	$_____
(check or money order—please do not send cash)	

To order, complete this form and send it, along with a check or money order
for the total above, payable to Harlequin Books, to: **In the U.S.:** 3010 Walden
Avenue, P.O. Box 9047, Buffalo, NY 14269-9047; **In Canada:** P.O. Box 613,
Fort Erie, Ontario, L2A 5X3.

Name: _____

Address: _____ City: _____

State/Prov.: _____ Zip/Postal Code: _____

*New York residents remit applicable sales taxes.
 Canadian residents remit applicable GST and provincial taxes.   HRCEBACK2

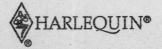

HARLEQUIN®